# At Death's Door...
# With a Will to Live

# At Death's Door...
# With a Will to Live

## Based on a True Story

## Betty Sue Houle

Faith Books, Inc.

*At Death's Door…With a Will to Live*
Copyright © 2010 Betty Sue Houle
Published by Faith Books, Inc.

All rights reserved. No part of this book may be reproduced (except for inclusion in reviews), disseminated or utilized in any form or by any means, electronic or mechanical, including photocopying, recording, or in any information storage and retrieval system, or the Internet/World Wide Web without written permission from the author or publisher.

For more information please contact:
houledavenport@aol.com

Book design by:
Arbor Books, Inc.
www.arborbooks.com

Printed in the United States of America

*At Death's Door…With a Will to Live*
Betty Sue Houle

1. Title   2. Author   3. Fiction

Library of Congress Control Number: 2009941084

ISBN 10: 0615335926
ISBN 13: 978-0-615-33592-6

*To my two sons who are the heroes in my life.
To my family and friends who prayed for me every day.
Your faith in God and His Love is what brought me through.
To my wonderful husband I just want to tell you how glad
I am that God blessed my life with you.*

# Chapter One

Connie Jo Filer did not know what to do with her hands. One moment she had them held tightly around her body as if to hold her insides together, followed a moment later by folding them crossed across her chest, a pouting, angry child. This would be followed by the erratic rhythms of reaching out to touch Ben's arm or chest, not necessarily with great passion but with a melancholy, as if she felt in her heart that this would be the last time she might ever see him. After that, the hands would be shoved into her pants pockets, as if to imprison them so they could not betray her displeasure by showing heartfelt love and affection.

"Stop that, now," Ben said gently, trying to reach out and hold on to one of those flailing hands, attempting to catch it before it went back into a pocket or became rigid in defiance. "I'll be all right. This is good. This is the best thing that could ever happen to us. This is an opportunity, and you know what they say about when opportunity knocks…"

Connie Jo's eyes teared, as much from brokenheartedness as from anger and disappointment. To an onlooker, it might have appeared as though they were two lovers in the midst of a quarrel or a breakup—the woman scorned yet still wishing it all away, and the man trying to say, "C'mon, can't we still be friends?"

"Saudi Arabia?! Saudi Arabia?!" Connie Jo repeated the words, just as she had been doing so for the past month, each time substituting them for a full explanation of their meaning. "Saudi Arabia" became code for, "Are you out of your mind? What are you thinking? Do you think you're single, that you don't have a family and you can just run off like a free bird of some sort? What about us? What about me and the kids?"

Ben had tired of it all, and yet his displeasure never showed. He stood near the boarding counter in the airline terminal. The gray, metallic door behind him had finally opened and the uniformed flight attendant began welcoming passengers with a smile and an outstretched hand collecting tickets.

Connie Jo's nose was red from crying, and yet there was a strength to her, a defiance. "This is crazy. This is a bad, bad idea."

"Shhh," said Ben. "If anything is going to happen, it's

going to happen here or wherever I am. When it's your time to go, no matter where you are, God is going to take you on."

"Don't talk like that, Ben. Don't talk like that."

"Well, it's you who's *boo hoo hoo*ing all over the place. Outside of me and this plane plopping down into the ocean, what else could you be worrying about? I'm just like any other man going off to work, that's all. Only difference is, I won't be coming back for a year. But I'll be sending you money; you know that. Lots of money. I ain't found anything back here in the States that pays anywhere near what this job in the desert pays. These American companies need engineers over there and they're willing to pay top dollar. They got good benefits and all of it is tax free."

Connie Jo sniffled. "We…We could tighten our belts. I could take on a second job. I could maybe ask my momma to watch the boys, or maybe we could even move in with them or something. I don't know."

"Connie Jo," said Ben, "we don't live high and mighty. We just want to live nice. We *ought* to live nice. And both of us have been willing to work for it. That's good—that's a good thing. We ain't been looking for a handout, and putting all sorts of pressure on your folks is a handout. I won't do it. I'm a man. This is my job. Look at it this way—going here for year, maybe that's working smart, not just working hard. We've just been working hard for nine years. Now we finally caught a break. God's watching over us. We both prayed on this and you know this is the right thing to do."

"I do not. This is not the right thing. A husband is supposed to be with his wife and kids. You're abandoning us. That's what it is—abandonment." Connie Jo's entire body stiffened in defiance. Still, Ben would not budge, would not let himself get dragged down into a mud fight.

"I ain't gonna be angry with you, darlin'. I know you're mad at me right now, but I ain't gonna let the last moments we spend together for a year be spent fussing."

Ben smiled, which only made Connie Jo angrier. She wanted him to get mad; she wanted him to start raising his voice. Maybe if he did that, he'd get angry enough to say, "To hell with it. Fine then, I'll stay home. I'll draw unemployment. I'll go on the dole. We'll sell the house. What do I care?" And Connie Jo would let him vent and while he did, she'd secretly smile because this was what she wanted. Yes, she wanted nice things and money; what young couple with two little boys didn't? But never had she dreamed she'd be all by herself, raising a family on her own, while her husband went off to another continent. This was like marrying a military man at a time of war, and Connie Jo hadn't done that, hadn't bought in to such an arrangement. This had not been part of the bargain when she'd married Ben Filer nine years earlier. Better, worse, richer, poorer; no one had said anything about alone and lonely, living like a single person.

Finally, Connie Jo found a pose she could live with. Hands on her hips, she glared at Ben, and no more words were necessary for him to understand her disagreement and disappointment in him.

"Connie Jo, I'm doing this for us. I'm doing it for you. I'm doing it for the boys. I told you, if you wanted, I could see if y'all could move out there with me."

"I ain't moving to no Saudi Arabia with my children, you can forget that," Connie Jo explained.

"Well then." Ben backed up a bit and looked at his young bride. Short, slender, blond, cute and spunky, she was indeed a pistol, every bit his match and his equal. Damn, how he loved her. He smiled at her, but she would not break character. She just did not know when to give up. Here he was, about two seconds away from stepping onto the plane, and she was somehow bound and determined to get him to chuck it all and reverse his plans. No, it wasn't going to happen, but he had to admire her persistence, no matter how much grief she was giving him.

This was a fine woman. Some frail flower would not have been able to handle being a single parent for a year, with those high-spirited preschoolers running all over the house. But he knew she was cut out for the job. This fussing and fighting they'd been going through, this was all the more reason why he knew she could handle it, despite her protestations to the contrary.

The final boarding call went out over the loudspeaker and Ben looked up at the ceiling as if he half expected to see a human being up there calling to him instead of a metal speaker countersunk into the acoustic tiles. Connie Jo's head did not move. She'd found her spot and she was going to stare Ben Filer out the door and all the way out until his airplane disappeared into the cloudless, blue, Alabama sky.

"It's time," Ben said, and still, Connie Jo did not move. Her mother and twin sister hung in the background, afraid to get mixed up in the middle of this domestic drama. They'd left B.J. and Gabriel, their two boys, at home, Connie Jo fearing how upset they'd be driving out to the airport and seeing their daddy go off on an airplane without them. That would be too much. So, Ben had said his good-byes to them at home, telling them both, "Now, who're you gonna listen to?"

"Momma," they'd both said in unison.

"And who's the boss?" he'd asked.

"Momma," they'd replied.

"And who's gonna bring you back lots of presents when he gets home?" he'd asked finally.

"Daddy!" they'd exclaimed as he'd bent down so they could both wrap their little arms around his neck.

Ben looked uncomfortable now, hoping against hope that Connie Jo would relent and give him a break. He didn't think she was cold and hard; no, just stubborn. And he knew her soft side. He knew that down underneath this spitfire exterior there was a soft, loving woman who'd spent much of the last month and all of that very day crying. She was tough, but inside she was as soft as banana cream pudding, and she loved him with all of her heart.

"I'm kissing you now," he said, and he did, "and I'm loving you," and he kissed her again, "and I'm already missing you," and he kissed her once more. Connie Jo, for her part, tried with all the strength within her to keep those hands steady on her hips and not give in to wrapping him up in the most passionate embrace she could muster, but she would not give him the satisfaction. Sometimes, a man had to know he was being punished, even if it was out of love.

Ben backed away and gave her a wink as one solitary tear rolled down Connie Jo's face. "You can beat me up when I come home loaded with money." Ben smiled and tried to get a laugh out of her, but all he saw were more tears, for which he felt awful. But still, he had a duty and like a soldier, he marched onto the plane and off to lands unknown, throwing a wave at his mother-in-law and sister-in-law, who were also crying, for they loved him so.

The last thing he did as he disappeared past the metal door leading to the airplane was look his wife in the eye and mouth the words, "I love you."

# Chapter Two

After two weeks alone, Connie Jo Filer received her first letter from her husband, Ben. It was less a letter than a blooming word bouquet, professing and re-professing his love to her. Still, Connie Jo would not be so easily swayed, although Ben's efforts were extraordinary for such a normally non-effusive man's man. She responded amicably enough, yet inserted the proverbial dagger when appropriate:

"I am trying my best with the boys and the bills, but it is all quite overwhelming, as I would hope you can imagine."

His letter in response came a few days later:

"Baby, the bills are going to be paid. I'll be getting paid and sending you some money very soon, I promise you. We are going to be living fine. All we needed was this little plug for us. This job is going to help me provide for you and the children the way I want to."

Connie Jo read it and rolled her eyes. "The check's in the mail," she muttered to herself.

She continued working at a local florist, making arrangements, and saving even more money by relying upon her sisters and mother to watch little B.J. and even littler Gabe rather than using the housekeeper-slash-babysitter she'd been using. Each day, she strode to the mailbox and almost every day there was another letter from Ben, each more loving than the last, but still, no check. She couldn't keep up the standoffish stance she'd taken with him; he sounded lonely and, most certainly, she felt that same way.

Theirs had been a good marriage, a strong marriage. They both had married young and they'd certainly had a lot to work out, trying to get used to the compromises marriage requires. Young people are rarely adept at compromise. But their values had been similar, as were their backgrounds. Both their families had been churchgoing folks, Southern Baptists from Alabama. Although they'd ended up moving to the city of Montgomery for work opportunities, both had grown up on the red-clayed, dusty roads of the country, where every neighbor *was* a neighbor and everybody knew everybody else. As much as they fussed and fumed at times, neither one of them dreamed for an instant that they wouldn't stay together forever and ever, amen.

One Sunday afternoon after church, there was a knock on Connie Jo's door. Getting up off the floor from playing with her boys, she straightened herself up for guests. Outside the door stood two men of dour countenances and behind them, her mother-in-law. Connie Jo did not get a good look at her mother-in-law's face, but if she had done so, she immediately would have known something was wrong.

"Mrs. Filer?" said the first man.

"Yes, that's me."

"I'm from Taylor Construction."

She thought, *Maybe they're here with some money. We sure could use it.*

He continued, "We need to talk to you."

The faces of the two men were funereal, and upon inviting them inside her home, Connie Jo could not yet see that her mother-in-law had been crying.

"Sit down, please. Boys, y'all go on upstairs and play for a while. We got grown-up things to talk about down here." Both boys dutifully left. Connie Jo immediately turned to the men and said, "What's the matter? I can tell something's the matter."

The first man rolled his tongue around the inside of his mouth to wet it and began what appeared to be a speech he'd been preparing all day long. "Ma'am, there was an accident on the worksite your husband, Ben, was at. Somehow, a large machine started up behind him when he was looking the other way. It had a big, movable blade and the blade hit him on the back of the head. He never knew what hit him—he never knew. He never felt the pain because it happened so quickly."

The conclusion of the story was missing. Connie Jo stared at the man with her mouth open, no words able to come out. She kept waiting for him to finish, to say what the upshot of it all was. The silence in the room was interminable. Where once he had been looking right into her eyes, his face now drooped noticeably, his eyes shifting downwards, hoping he would not have to complete his own thought.

For her part, Connie Jo refused to give in to the obvious; she knew why he could go no further, but maybe, just maybe, if nothing more was said, God would make it all not so.

Finally, Connie Jo's mother-in-law could no longer stand the inconclusiveness of the moment. "Ben's dead," she cried as whatever tears were left in her body came exploding out once more. Her face crinkled up and reddened, inconsolable.

Connie Jo continued to sit in utter shock. She said not a word. She wrestled life itself to determine whether this was all a dream or a bad joke. Maybe if she said nothing, maybe if she remained perfectly still, all these people would disappear and leave her home and everything would go back to normal—the kids would play, the television would come on, the house would be filled with normal, everyday sounds, and everything would be just so, just as it should be.

"Ben's dead!" Maddy Filer cried again, and this time it was not to be ignored. Connie Jo stared into the face of the man who had spoken, then to his silent partner, who seemed simply glad to have not been the one to have to tell the tale. Both men quietly and wordlessly nodded as Maddy Filer wept. Yes, the woman was telling the truth. Yes, she had lost her beloved son, a pain worse than any pain a person could ever be asked to endure. Perhaps it was this realization, amidst the confusion and unbelievability, that was the only thing that kept Connie Jo from immediately losing all control as well. Maddy had beaten her to it. Maddy had a lost a son. No parent should ever have to endure such a thing.

Connie Jo stared at the men, at Maddy, at the door, the floor, the window and the walls. Ben was dead; Ben was dead. Her face was wet with tears she did not even know she was creating.

Still wordless, Connie Jo thought to herself, *He's not dead yet. He's almost dead, but there's still time. There's still time to talk to him one more time, to tell him everything I feel for him, to let him know he's been a wonderful husband and father and that we all need him to watch over us and care for us. There's still time for him to talk one more time to me, to tell me I'm his special girl and that I mean the world to him. There's still time to tie up all our loose ends and make everything right.* But there was no time. Time had slipped away. Ben was dead. Ben was dead.

## Chapter Three

It took ten days for Ben Filer's body to be shipped from Saudi Arabia to the USA, time enough to make the grieving unbearable for a young woman and her two little boys. Connie Jo was in a state of shock, barely able to function. *I never got to say good-bye. The last moments I spent with him, he thought I was angry with him,* was all she could think.

With his body came his belongings. The company men had been so careful to say how quickly he'd died and how he had not felt a thing, had not suffered. Yet inside his pants was a pocket watch, and it had been crushed, decimated. In their version of the fatal events, they had tried to soften the blow, to spare his young wife, but in the end it had been unsuccessful.

Connie Jo's family came to her side, as she expected they

would, for they were a close, close family. They took her to her family physician, Dr. Morris, who prescribed sedatives to help ease her suffering. "When the body arrives, Connie Jo, I want you to view it. I know you're having a tough time of it, but you'll not be able to set your mind at rest until you see with your own eyes that Ben is gone and he ain't coming back."

"But they told us to have a closed casket service, Dr. Morris. They said he doesn't look right. I know they said he didn't suffer, but I think they were lying. There must be something terrible for me to see or else they'd let everybody see him and pay their respects."

"I'll request they open the casket for you, Connie Jo," he said. "I'll sign off on it, saying it's in the best interest of your mental health. It's like the old hymn 'Will the Circle Be Unbroken'—'You can picture happy gatherings 'round the fireside long ago, and you think of tearful partings when they left you here below. One by one their seats were emptied, one by one they went away. Here the circle has been broken—Will it be complete one day?'"

Connie Jo sniffled. "It's my fault. It's all my fault. If I hadn't wanted so much, Ben would still be here. I did this to him. When I look at him, that's all I'm going to think."

"Hush, now. That's how you feel already. You've got to close the circle. You've got to embrace this and move on. You've got two young boys depending on you. I'm trying to give you the best advice I can so you can be strong for those boys," said Dr. Morris. "You have to be strong again for them."

As much sense as it made, and as caring and kind as the old doctor was, the act itself was horrific. Ben had been dead for too long, and was unprepared for viewing. Less than thirty years old, he looked like he was ninety. They could not put a suit on him; they had him zipped up in a plastic bag inside the coffin. Connie Jo had brought along a suit his family had provided, but looking at Ben the way he was, it was useless and worthless to even try.

The sight of her loving husband in such a way left Connie Jo scarred and shaken. The image burned itself into her brain.

After the closed-casket funeral, folks came on by, but Connie Jo was like a toy with its batteries pulled out, a damp dishrag of a woman, barely able to hold her head up to accept heartfelt sympathies from family, neighbors and friends.

A few days later, a letter arrived from Saudi Arabia. Connie Jo's heart quickened as she hoped it might be some last message from Ben, something to complete her circle, to make things right within her. But she had already received Ben's last missive. It had been nice, as all of them were, but like all the others, it had no sense of finality. It simply contained words written by a man who felt he had an entire lifetime ahead of him. If he only had known…

This letter was from a coworker of Ben's, a man Connie Jo had never before met or even heard of. The note said, "Ben was a good old boy. He was so good that everybody called him 'good old Ben.' Mrs. Filer, I want you to know that the night before he died, he had his mind on his family, the most precious and dear thing to him. That's what he said to me, and I wanted you to know that right up until the moment he died, you and your boys were always on his mind. Nothing was more important to him."

## Chapter Four

For the next ten months, Connie Jo retreated into herself, totally withdrawing from people as much as possible. As for the money the Filers so sorely needed, it now was there. The irony of Ben's accident was that with insurance, worker's compensation and whatnot, Connie Jo was suddenly and unexpectedly set for life. No, she could not afford to live like an heiress in a mansion, but outside of that, everything was set. She had a home, she had savings and she had income. If she didn't want to, she did not need to work again for the rest of her life. That being said, she gave up her job and dedicated herself to trying to be the best mother she possibly could.

B.J. and Gabe enrolled in preschool and missed their daddy. But the sorrow of a child of four or five is transient.

There were games to play, television to watch and noise to make. The voids in their hearts would fill and heal. Eventually, they would forget, but Connie Jo would not.

Staying in the house she and Ben had purchased in Montgomery suited her now. When he had moved to Saudi Arabia, there had been a pull to go back to where she'd been raised, about thirty miles away, to be closer to her folks. But now, she appreciated that they could not be with her as often as they would have liked. Connie Jo was punishing herself.

*If I had only been a better wife. I did this to him. I killed him. I wanted too much. I needed too much. I was a selfish woman. If I could only bring him back, I could make this right. I understand now my priorities in life. I had it all—I had my family, my boys, my faith and my husband. Money…money is a terrible thing. Look what money did to my Ben.*

But Ben wasn't coming back.

Connie Jo knew very few people in Montgomery and at this point in her life she liked it that way. The only people visiting her were family, when they could manage to ride on out to see her, and the minister of the local church she had begun attending upon moving with Ben to Montgomery. The preacher and his wife came over quite often and they soon became Connie Jo's best and only friends. And yet, this only created more internal conflict and guilt.

*God, why did you have to take him away? Why did he have to go? He had two small children. He had a wife who loved him and he was a good man. In this world, there are people who are so bad, and they're still living. Why did you have to take Ben? Why?*

⌒⁄⌒

"Connie Jo, you've been sitting here dying more and more each day. I see Exa getting a smile and a little life out of you once you let your defenses down, but that ain't enough," said Pastor Shirey one day as he and his wife sat on Connie Jo's living room sofa while her boys played upstairs.

Connie Jo responded, "Oh, I love when you two come out to see me. You're the only ones. I think that when I see my own family—my own family!—it just makes me think all the more about dear Ben. But you two, you're my breath of fresh air. You're my new light. How can I ever repay you?"

"Connie Jo, you don't owe us anything. We owe you. That's how God works. We've all been charged with spreading love to our neighbors in need," Exa Shirey exclaimed. "The Lord sent me this fine man when *my* first husband died." Vardemen Shirey blushed and waved away his plump, cheery-faced spouse. "Honey, you need to get out of here. Now, I know, we've been saying this for a long time now. And all you've been talking about is how much your family has been getting on your last nerve by doing the same thing. So, before you throw us both out of your fine home, shut us all up by doing something. Rise up! Rise up and walk!" Exa Shirey chuckled her infectious laugh, and soon Connie Jo couldn't help but join in.

"I've got an idea, Connie Jo. Vardemen, didn't you say you could use some extra help down at the church?"

"Oh, darlin', now you're putting me on the spot," he laughed. "No, no really, I could. I could use another set of hands a couple-a days a week. Connie Jo, you don't have to make a big commitment. Two, maybe three days a week or so, you just come on in and I'll put those idle hands of yours to work for the Lord. I know you've been troubled through all this and maybe you've got to get out of here and back into the church more so you can make yourself right with the Savior. Get closer to Him and find a peace in your heart so you can ask His blessings upon your precious children. Will you think about it?"

Honestly, it was the best and most appealing offer anyone had made to her and being in the funk she was, nothing better appeared to be emanating from within her own brain. Connie Jo relented and soon she was attending services at the church on Sundays, Sunday nights and Wednesdays, and working in the church office with Exa Shirey a few other days in between. At first, she stayed to herself, clinging to Exa and her good-natured ways the way a shy child would hide behind her mother's apron. This behavior was so unlike her, so different from how she had been growing up, so different from how she had been with Ben. He wouldn't have recognized her behavior, she'd been so devastated.

Eventually, the healing the Shireys had spoken of began to take hold. She was still not her old self, but she was able to take solace again in the church, and regretted and retracted the doubts she'd ever had about her Lord and Savior.

One day, after a particularly fulfilling week wherein she'd thrown herself wholeheartedly into church activities, she began to feel guilt—but it was a new guilt, different than the guilt she had been obsessed with due to Ben's untimely passing. She drove on down to the church on a day and time when she was not expected. She was pleased to find Vardemen and Exa together in the office, with no one else around.

"Well, well, looky here. First we had to drag her out of her house and now we can't get rid of her!" Vardemen guffawed and Exa slapped him playfully as she joined in.

As much fun as they both were, sometimes the sight of them made Connie Jo wistful. *Now this is a marriage. These two were made together for each other in heaven. I once had that and then I lost it. Oh, why, God, why?*

Connie Jo composed herself as if she were about to give an important speech. "I just want you two to know something. You two remind me of the Book of Matthew. 'When I was a stranger, you took me in, and when I was sick, you visited me.' It seems that all I've been doing is taking and taking. That's not right. I am so happy that you brought me back to the church. I needed to be back in this environment. It suits me. It nourishes me."

"Amen," said Vardemen solemnly.

"I want to keep working here, if you'll have me. But more than that, I need to share with the church as the church has shared with me. Ben left me and the boys properly taken care of financially, and now you and the church have taken care of me spiritually. I just went down to the bank and took out a ten-thousand-dollar CD I want to tithe to the building fund in Ben's memory."

Brother Vardemen was taken aback, speechless. Exa's face filled with love and joy as she got up out of her chair and threw her arms around her new friend. "Oh, Connie Jo, Connie Jo! I knew the moment I met you you were a righteous woman. God bless you, darlin'. God bless you. May all good things come to you."

# Chapter Five

"You have to get out more, Connie Jo. You're dying on the vine," Exa Shirey said with equal parts enthusiasm and frustration.

"Exa, I'm spending near all my time here at the church. What more do you want from me?" said Connie Jo as she folded bulletins for next Sunday's service. "You're a worse nag than a puppy that has to go outside."

Exa Shirey stopped her work and turned to her friend. "You know what I mean, Miss Missy. You're far too young to be turning into 'the widow Filer.' Pretty soon you'll be wearing black all day long and talking to a house full of cats. You need a fella in your life. Why, I'd think I died and went to heaven if I had a figure nice as yours. Vardemen would think *he* died and went to heaven, too," she laughed.

Connie Jo blushed as she continued folding. "Oh, you're just trying to embarrass me. It's only been a year. What would people think? What would my children think—me going out and trying to replace their daddy? It's not right."

The soft, round Exa rolled her chair over closer to her friend. "Listen," she whispered, "I have a cousin. He's a handsome man and he's coming up to visit from Georgia next week for the revival. I've been telling him about you and he wants to meet you."

Connie Jo slapped her hand down on her stack of church bulletins. "Exa! Why'd you go and do a thing like that? I'm not ready for such a thing. I have no interest in men!"

"Well, honey, men have an interest in you—I can see that with my own eyes. God doesn't hate them for that, and God wouldn't hate you for looking up from your work long enough to notice it and do something about it. He didn't mean for you to spend the rest of your life in penance. I know you still blame yourself for Ben's death, but you were a million miles away. You were no more to blame for what happened than I was. Besides which, what I didn't happen to mention is that the reason he's coming in for the revival is 'cause he's preaching at it. The man's a Christian minister. Now, if that's not a sign from God, I'm gonna have to set a bush on fire or part the sea to open your eyes!"

For the first time, Connie Jo allowed her mouth to curl into a slight smile. "A preacher?" She paused a moment, mulling it over. "It still isn't right. I'm not ready to meet nobody just yet. It wouldn't look right. It doesn't feel right. But I thank you for thinking about me. You're kind."

"Little girl, when the time comes, the Lord will allow you to have the feelings that you need to have for when you start dating or have any kind of relationship that you feel like you need. God will give you peace about it."

The morning of the revival, Exa Shirey was at it again, undeterred. "Connie Jo, you look good tonight. You recall who I said was gonna be here. And he's still interested in meeting you. I told him you were reluctant, but he's a fine man of the cloth and when I described you to him, he thought you sounded like you were put on Earth just for him."

"Exa Shirey, I'm gonna kill you, I swear! What've you been telling this poor man? I'll never live up to your exaggerations!"

"Sister, more than anything else, I've been telling him about your situation and about you and your boys and how you've spent the past few months toiling away in our church, and how you even gave some of your inheritance to help us out. I told him you were the finest Christian woman I'd ever met, and I mean that. You're a catch, I swear." Exa paused. "And I told him you looked like one of the Mandrell sisters."

"Exa Shirey!"

"Connie Jo, you just promise me you won't run off as soon as the revival's over. And pay attention to my cousin's message. His name is Brother Delbert Mobley—we all call him 'Del.' He's been having hard times lately himself, and he needs to find himself a sweet lady friend, and you ought to be meeting a nice man friend. I'm not trying to push you two into marriage or anything, God forbid. I just think that if you'd stop and get to know one another, you could be company for each other. What's wrong with that?"

Connie Jo was wearing down. "Look, you know I'll be at the revival, so I'll make you a promise I won't go on home before you have a chance to introduce me. I'll meet the man, but that's all I'll promise—nothing more."

That evening, Del Mobley took the stage and Connie Jo sized the man up. Handsome. He cut a figure like a real man, a tall, strong, broad-shouldered, broad-chested fellow with auburn hair. He started off slowly, joshing with Vardemen Shirey, the two men doing a humorous give and take, old friends glad to see one another again. But after Vardemen left the stage, Del Mobley took over like no one Connie Jo ever had seen in her life. Del Mobley stalked the stage like a lion, his flowing, auburn mane following him as he whipped around and cut the air with his voice and with his hands. This was fire-and-brimstone preaching at its most theatrical and the entire congregation was spellbound.

Who was this Del Mobley character? From what planet had he come? After the initial shock wore off, the amazement that had sent the congregants upright in their seats, heads back, chins upward, they began to respond like a Roman chorus. They needed no prompting, no rehearsal, when Brother Del simply drew from their throats a chorus of spontaneous "amen!"s or forceful applause. His mighty arms pointed right at them where they sat, or gestured high into heaven. His suit jacket fell from his shoulder, no longer able to contain the athlete's body that propelled it like it was a shackle he needed to flick from his hide.

He would stop for a moment as if to give the audience—not himself, but the audience—a chance to catch its collective breath, which it did with applause and more applause. Only then did he look down and away from them, a show of humility amidst the adulation. *He's giving it up for God,* Connie Jo thought. *This man is the Lord's own instrument.*

No sooner had he riled everyone up than he took them down with him, lowering his voice to a stage whisper, and they, too, grew silent. *This is like making love,* Connie Jo thought, and never before had she made such a parallel. Brother Del was treating the audience like a woman—seducing her, enrapturing her, strutting his maleness and yet lifting her high upon a pedestal, as all women wish to be praised.

In a lifetime of churchgoing, she had never felt this this melding of sex and solemnity. This man had total control over his voice as well as his body, both of them spiritual instruments designed to plunge deep into the recesses of the soul, rising up and letting down. Never before had Connie Jo Filer felt anything such as this in a house of worship. Emotions rushed through her body like a levee overflowing. She felt her face redden and flush. She was at once filled with the Holy Spirit and some strange and incredible feeling she could not explain. She felt embarrassed that this man, this mortal man, could have this effect on her.

When she tried to look around, for it was nearly impossible to take her eyes off of Brother Del Mobley as he preached, she saw that it was not just her, but every human being in the audience. Old men and young children appeared to be feeling exactly as she did, and this alone allowed her to succumb to the final release of any inhibitions and embarrassment she felt. When Brother Del's message was over, he was spent, as was she and everyone else in attendance.

Afterwards, Exa Shirey sought her out, excitedly waving Connie Jo to her side. "C'mon, c'mon now. I want you to meet somebody." There was no surprise in who this somebody would be. No, from the moment he had finished his sermon, all Connie Jo Filer could think about was how on Earth she would or could face this man, this heavenly celebrity. What could you say to one of God's own disciples? Surely he could not be like Vardemen Shirey or any other preacher she had ever heard, and there had been many before this night in Connie Jo's life. They had been mere men, fellows you could sit down and chat with over a soda pop and a plate of cookies. This Delbert Mobley could not be like that, as normal and unassuming as they.

Connie Jo shuffled along, trepidant and scared. The crowd parted and there he was, tall as she'd expected, looming over her like a statue rather than a man. He smiled a kind smile, filled with sincerity and—could it be humility, almost shyness? In that moment, she was not only in awe, but for some strange reason, she was empathetic, as if he had something about him one wanted to mother or comfort.

*He needs me,* she thought. *I don't know why, but for some reason, he needs me, and here I am.*

Gallantly, he extended his meaty, soft, right hand. "Hi, Connie. Cousin Exa's told me a lot about you. I'm Del Mobley."

# Chapter Six

After a few moments of chitchat during which Connie Jo felt alternately awkward and unusually comfortable, Del Mobley said, "Connie, I'd like to take you out to Shoney's for a cup of coffee or maybe a bite to eat—whatever you want to do. I would really like to get to know you."

For a moment, Connie Jo Filer was speechless. It had been hard enough just talking with this man in the midst of others who had gathered around him at the end of services. Yet in those few public moments, she had seen even more sides to the man, sides that were not even shown on stage, when he was running the emotional gamut, as he rallied men, women and children to Jesus. In an instant, he would vacillate between awkward, self-effacing and shy to glorious and gregarious. He was at once a needy, lonely child and a giant statue of ferocious manliness. It all made Connie Jo's knees buckle.

"I…I can't. I have my children with me," she said as she draped her arms around B.J. and Gabe.

Exa Shirey piped up. "My sister lives out by you, honey. Rowena would be happy to give them a ride home, tuck them in bed and stay with them until you get home, won't you Rowena?"

The woman, whom Connie Jo knew casually, nodded in assent.

Connie Jo had fired her best shot, trying to blame her discomfort on her children, and now she felt helpless, still reluctant to take this first step forward toward the beginning of her new life. *It's wrong! Ben's body is hardly cold. What will people think?*

"Th-that's kind of you, Rowena, but I just don't know. It wouldn't…It wouldn't…" She so desperately wanted to say, "It wouldn't look right," but she was acutely aware of how insulting that could sound. He was a preacher. He wasn't asking her to some sleazy motel or even a dark nightclub. A cup of coffee—how could she refuse?

"Listen," said Exa Shirey, "Let's make it a foursome. Vardemen and I wanted to catch up some with Brother Del anyway, so this will just make it more pleasant. Connie Jo, I want your company—you're my best friend. Please, come with us. I'll ride with you, and you can give me a lift while the two preachers ride together and argue about scripture." She smiled.

How could Connie Jo refuse? Still, the entire time she was riding along in her car with Exa Shirey, she tuned the happy woman out, deep within her own thoughts. *It isn't a date—it's coffee with some church friends, that's all. Besides, he couldn't be interested in me. He's...He's this magnificent, special man and I'm just little ol' me. Life wasn't set out for me that way. In a million years, no man like Reverend Delbert Mobley would look upon me as his special partner in life. He needs a woman equal to him, someone who would shine next to him. I can't see myself in those shoes. That's too much.*

Over coffee, Del Mobley fawned over Connie Jo like an ambitious suitor, speaking just enough with Vardemen and Exa so that they would not find him rude. But his entire focus that evening was Connie Jo Filer. Every moment, he gazed into her eyes. His blue eyes drilled right into her soul. It was as flattering as it was disconcerting.

Connie Jo had never felt so self-conscious in her entire life. Ben had never made her feel this way. Ben had been a good old boy, a nice, sweet man. The two of them had grown up together, learned the lessons of life with one another, stumbled and fell in front of each other and laughed together as they'd both made the mistakes every human makes. They'd been like staggering fawns, learning together how to walk and run. But Del Mobley, he was a man of the world. He was complete.

Was Connie Jo? Was she complete? She knew she didn't feel complete, not with Ben gone from her life. But aside from that, she doubted herself more with this man than at any other moment in her life. *Who am I? Where am I headed next? Where will I be next month, next year, ten years from now?*

Connie Jo had not stopped to think about any of these things during her time of mourning. When she had been with Ben, it had all been so simple—she and Ben would raise their boys and they would be together always and forever, period. But now that plan was trashed, cut down in some far-off country. Only now did Connie Jo realize that she had no plan B.

Outside of the intense and obviously lustful stares of Del Mobley, there were also the words. Oh, how his words sang, just like when he preached. "Connie, are you dating anyone?"

"No," she replied.

"I can't believe it. You're just too fine and pretty not to be dating anyone. You're a very sweet person."

"Brother Del…" she began.

"Just Del. When we're outside of church, it's just Del to you, darlin'."

"Del…you don't even know me."

"I'm good at judging people. I'm an expert at determining character and you, little miss, are a fine lady, I can just tell that. I know it every time I look into your eyes. The eyes don't lie, you know? The eyes tell you everything." And it seemed like he'd said it just as another excuse to stare deeply into Connie Jo's eyes once more, as if he'd finally asked permission and that permission had been granted by silent agreement. Never before had Connie Jo Filer felt so publicly and respectfully seduced.

Finally, it came time to leave. As was done on every first date, Connie Jo wondered what would come next. But no, this wasn't a date, because she could not date, would not date. That decision was one she had come to terms with firmly. She wasn't ready; she doubted she might ever be ready. This was coffee and cake with friends from church. That a handsome stranger had sat across from her and gazed into her eyes and complimented her was nothing more than a wonderful fantasy she could relive in her daydreams, nothing more than that.

"Connie, I'd like to call you sometime," said Del Mobley.

"Well, sure," she replied without thinking. It came out of her mouth thoughtlessly, the way people say, "How are you?" And no matter what the truth is, you always answer, "Fine, and you?" It was automatic, but now she regretted it. Before she could clarify or retract it, he was gone.

# Chapter Seven

"Connie Jo, Del just called me today and he said he's driving up here from Georgia on Saturday and for me to have you here. He said he wants to take you out to dinner and wants to go out with you," said Exa Shirey excitedly.

Connie Jo opened her mouth to speak, then thought for a moment so she would not say something impulsively. Del Mobley had been on her mind since the previous Sunday night; in fact, nothing else but Del Mobley had been in her thoughts. Had that night even occurred, or was it just a dream? Somehow, without it having been an actual date with a man, it had been the most romantic evening she had ever spent. Never before had she been so mesmerized, so thoroughly swept off her feet, and yet it all had been so safe, so proper. They'd spent an evening under bright, fluorescent lights, drinking nothing stronger than decaf coffee, along with another minister and his wife as well as numerous other acquaintances who had stopped on by to pay their respects to the out-of-town stranger.

"Exa, I just don't think I'm ready for that right now."

Exa Shirey rolled her eyes heavenward and came closer. "Listen, he's driving over here and I would hate for you to let him down. He's a fine fellow, Connie. He's a minister and he's my first cousin. Men like Del don't come along every day. If you let him out of your sight, you'll regret it once you finally come around. He'll be long gone."

Connie Jo felt pressured, but more by logic than by Exa Shirey or Del Mobley. "Look, I'll do it on one condition. You and Vardemen have to come with us again."

Exa snickered. "So Vardemen and I have to be your chaperones. Alright then. I never thought of you as my virtuous daughter, but if that's the role you want to play, I'll play along. It's downright laughable, but I'm always up for some silliness and this is about as silly as it gets. Woman here is afraid some Baptist minister is gonna knock her down and pounce on her like a wild man fresh out of prison. Well, alright then."

Indeed, Connie Jo felt a bit foolish, but her heart was torn. *Couldn't he come around later? Some other time? Maybe in another year or two, maybe longer? I don't know. Why do I still fell so darn guilty, so sad?* she thought.

Connie Jo prepared herself this time as if it were a

real date, forcing herself by doing so to confront her own demons. She dressed really nicely, brought out her favorite perfume and admired herself in the mirror. *I do look nice. I haven't hardly tried to look this nice in over a year. I am young. Why can't God grant me some absolution so that deep inside my soul I can move on with my life?*

Del, Connie Jo, Vardemen and Exa headed out for dinner at the Steak and Ale in Montgomery and had as good a time as they'd had the previous Sunday. It turned out that Vardemen and Del didn't know each other quite as well as Connie Jo had previously thought. But they joked and joshed and seemed to make a fine connection, just as Del continued his flirtatious ways around her.

There seemed to be less-intense staring this time, more acting like a pair of long-time couples out on a double date. It relaxed Connie Jo more, and she slowly began to let down her guard. She still didn't know that many people in Montgomery. So what if one of the few that she knew saw her like this? It had been over a year. She was a young woman, under thirty. And this was a man of God and they were out with another preacher and his wife. Things couldn't get more dignified.

"Let's go find someplace to play putt putt." Everyone had finished their dessert and Del Mobley took it upon himself to take charge of the group.

"Del, I'm in high heels!" said Connie.

"Yes, well, is that supposed to intimidate me? 'Cause if you think that will make you play better by making you taller, maybe I can swing by some shoe store and pick myself up a pair and I'll play better, too!"

Everyone at the table laughed. *My,* Connie Jo thought, *what an amazing manner this man has. He always knows the right thing to say to make me smile.*

The previous night they had been together, Connie Jo had gone over the obvious issue of the untimely demise of her Ben. Yet, she had not felt comfortable enough to ask Del Mobley the same question. "Del, are you married?"

"Why, no, of course not. What sort of man would be married to one woman and dating another?"

"We are not dating. We're just four people out having a meal and playing putt putt," Connie Jo replied.

"Well, except for the four people part, that sounds like a date to me," Del said with a smile. He and Connie Jo laughed as she struggled along, trying to play well in her high heels.

"Okay, so you're not married. But at your age, you can't tell me you've never *been* married," Connie Jo said, fishing for more information. If she were to have a true change of heart, she needed to know a number of things, and the best way to find things out as to just come right out and ask. Still, had it been anyone other than Del Mobley, that would have been easier. There was something about him that intimidated her, like she was out with a celebrity or something, and if she were to say the wrong thing and rub him the wrong way, he'd be out of her life for good, and this she did not want.

"Yes, I've been married. Got married a long time ago.

She's gone now." As he said it, he dropped his head almost as if in prayer.

*Oh my,* Connie Jo thought, *I've gone and taken him to a sad place. That must be why he's pursuing me. He's lonely, too.*

"Any little ones?" she asked.

Del hesitated only an instant and then answered strongly, "No, no little ones. What you see is what you get—just me here, all by my lonesome." And as he said it, he did sound awfully lonesome, yet prideful and dignified.

Maybe this was exactly what she needed, Connie Jo thought. Someone who'd been through a similar situation as she—a widower who had turned the corner and was ready to settle down. Suddenly, the thought of "dating around" repulsed Connie Jo even more than what she was doing now, going out on a double date with the Shireys. She'd been with this man twice now. No, it wasn't much, but it was consistent. No way was she going to start hanging out in singles bars and nightclubs.

This…This might have been the perfect situation, the perfect way to get back into life. This was exactly the sort of man she'd always hoped to meet, even before she had met Ben Filer. Ben had been a good man, and so was Del Mobley, but Del was a preacher and if she had a choice in vocation for the man of her dreams, that would have been it. Now, the most handsome, charismatic preacher she had ever before seen was chasing her as if he had to have her. Connie Jo allowed herself to drift into bliss.

# Chapter Eight

Del Mobley never went back to Georgia. For the next four weeks, he moved in with his cousin, Exa Shirey, and saw Connie Jo Filer every single night. At first, they continued to always have Vardemen and Exa by their sides, many times simply hanging out together at the Shirey's home, but eventually, Connie Jo allowed Del to escort her around Montgomery on a proper date, just the two of them.

The first true physical contact between them came after another night or two, much the way things tend to blossom. Del walked her to her door and respectfully bowed his head towards her, gently taking her chin between his thumb and index finger and lightly kissing her on the lips, then slowly withdrawing with a smile. Connie Jo flushed with feelings she had been repressing for what seemed like forever.

Whenever she thought of Del Mobley in a romantic or amorous way, she felt more embarrassed than she ever had felt in her life. This was not a retreat back to schoolgirl days of braces and pigtails but guilt, strong guilt that would not leave her be. *God, why do you taunt me in this way? Why did you bring this man into my life if I cannot give myself up to him? Why am I still imprisoned in my own mind and soul? Why?*

Slowly, gradually, Connie Jo prayed on the matter. She went down on her knees every night after seeing Del Mobley and asked God what it was He wanted from her, what the proper things to think and feel were.

A week or two later, things began to steam up more between them. They would never spend time at her place, as she felt it might confuse B.J. and Gabe, and so Vardemen and Exa Shirey opened up their home to both of them as if it were their own. It became a ritual for Exa Shirey to yawn and stretch her bulbous arms above her head and say, "Vardemen, I am just *so* tired, I don't know why. Come on up and tuck me into bed so I don't get lonely." She'd smile slyly at her husband and then at both Connie Jo and Del, winking as if the only one not privy to their secret was the clueless Brother Vardemen. Together, they would go upstairs to their bedroom, leaving Connie Jo and Del alone in the living room with the television on.

From there, it was like a scene out of high school. Del Mobley changed from the fire-and-brimstone preacher to the randy schoolboy, and Connie Jo Filer was the virtuous, virginal, pom-pom girl fighting him off, all the while trying hard not to turn him off so completely that he would lose all interest. It felt strange, this retreat to yesteryear. Connie Jo and Ben had experienced a wonderful, healthy love life, but that had been for Ben, her precious Ben; it was never meant to be for anyone else. Connie Jo still could not wrap her mind around the fact that Ben was gone, gone forever.

They'd never talked about death, she and Ben. They'd both been far too young. Even when they had the boys, they took out the requisite insurance policies, but still, it was an autonomic thing, just like filling out a tax return or getting a car inspection. It was just something you did because it was the grown-up thing to do, nothing more. There were no great discussions about death and wills and dying. Yes, they both knew they wouldn't live forever, but thoughts of death focused solely on the normal human fear of it and how they both assuaged their souls with the belief that God, hopefully, would judge them as good and would lead them into the promised land of heaven.

But the practical aspects of death, of what each wanted in terms of funerals, memorials, and how they wanted each other to carry forward alone—none of this had ever been discussed. Those were the conversations people their parents' ages had, not folks in their twenties like Connie Jo and Ben. *So what now, Ben? What do you want from me? What do I have your permission to think, do and feel? Are you right with this? What should I do?*

"Del!" Connie Jo cried out, her mouth muffled against his neck.

"What?" said Del Mobley dumbly, his voice quivering and croaking as sweat beaded up on his forehead.

"It's getting too much. I don't like it." Connie Jo pushed up against his chest, which pinned her on the Shireys' couch. His hands were everywhere and his passionate kisses seemed to be as much an attempt at subduing her, preventing her from protesting, as anything else.

"Connie, I can't go on without making love to you. I just can't. You make me crazy like no woman ever has."

"I don't care, Del. It isn't right. I'm not that kind of girl. We're not married. And we're on someone else's sofa and they're right upstairs."

Del Mobley remained on top of her, insistent. "We could go somewhere else. We could go to a motel."

"No! I'm not some sort of tramp," Connie Jo replied.

Despite the protestations, Del Mobley never lost his patience or persistence. "Connie, I haven't been with a woman in years. I want you so bad and I can't wait much longer. I have needs that have to be met and I've met someone who I want to share that with."

It had been a month in which they had seen each other nearly every night. Connie Jo had adjusted her thinking to allow her to be able to enjoy Del Mobley's constant company, but little more. The times they spent together were fun. Along with everything else, he was a joy to be with, a pleasant companion who always brightened her day. But beyond the immediate, she could not think far into the future. Each day was merely what it was—a morning, a daytime, time spent working around the house, taking care of her kids, working in the church with Exa, and each evening, seeing Del.

Del had become as routine as vacuuming the livingroom carpet and had, finally, become just as pedestrian. She enjoyed it far more than housework and there was definitely a passion to it, but she still could not fully commit herself to the passion. Had there never been a Ben Filer in her life, she would have thrown herself at Del Mobley as she had never before thrown herself at any man. But no longer did her mind work that way. In answer to the slings and arrows thrown her way by Exa Shirey, she had reached a state of contentment that she might stay just as she was—single—while the boys were still young enough to be living at home with her. That would be less confusing and tormenting.

Thinking back to her old single days—for despite Ben's passing, she did not quite think of herself as single—she found that some men seemed like they would make great husbands. Others had sparks about them that made her think they'd make wonderful fathers. But a man who could do both—that was a rarity.

Now that she had two sons, it was a much harder situation to face. Oh, how she feared she might ruin Ben's one great legacy—his sons. Every woman worries about being a good mother, but none as much as the woman who has to do it alone. This weighed on her. Sometimes, she had trouble convincing herself that they were actually her own children; she thought, rather, that they were Ben's children and she had been entrusted with them. She prayed for the lives of those boys every single night, not merely to keep them safe but for the guidance to steer them in the right direction and help them to become the kind of men of which Ben would be proud.

Del Mobley got up off the couch and said, "Don't get up. You stay right there." He arose and walked across the room, turning on the stereo. He then moved slowly over to the light switch, hitting the dimmer and creating a sensual, barely lit glow in the room. Del then left the room completely, returning with an armload of large pillows, coming before the sofa and dropping them upon the floor. "C'mon down here on the floor with me."

"I will not! I know what you're gonna do and it's just not right. We have to wait," said Connie Jo.

"For God's sake, Connie, I'm not going to do anything to you and I'm not going to hurt you. All I want to do is to show you something."

It sounded ominous, but still, part of Connie had grown to trust Del Mobley, the minister from Georgia, the man of God who preached with the voice of God Himself. She complied, and Del got down on the floor and lay down beside her, propping himself up on his elbow. He stared deeply into her eyes and said, "Connie, I love you and I want you to marry me." He reached into his pocket and pulled out a ring. "This ring was my mother's. She died only a few years ago and I'm an only child. I never thought I would meet a woman who would be worthy of wearing my momma's ring—that is, until I met you. I know you will be a good wife to me. I know you'll be good. I know you're good to your children and you would be an asset to me as a pastor's wife. Connie, I really need you. I need you as my wife and I need you in the ministry."

It was as if he could read her mind. Connie Jo Filer had not been wishing and hoping for a marriage proposal, but were she to ever again received one, this was exactly what she would want to hear. That fact alone made her forget for a moment how short a time it was since they had first laid eyes on one another. A minister's wife. Helping with his ministry. Being an instrument of God. Having a relationship with the sort of man Del Mobley was, in addition to finding him so very charismatic and handsome, intelligent and kind, funny and gregarious, giving and gallant. It was all too, too perfect.

"Del, you don't really know me well enough to ask me to marry you."

"Connie, all I know is that I love you and I need you and that's all that counts."

Connie Jo tried as hard as should could to digest it all, to collect herself, but it was oh, so difficult. She had to remain in the moment as well as in the past and future at the very same time. *Ben, is this what you want for me? God, is this your command?*

"My children…" she began.

"Your two boys need a father, Connie Jo. They shouldn't grow up without a man in the house. Who knows what will become of them in an environment like that? I know you're a good mother, but boys—boys, they need more than just a mother, even the best mother in the world. They need a father to keep them straight with the world and with the Lord. There are too many temptations you can't even begin to imagine. I'll help make sure they come out to be fine, strong men."

There was another side she saw to him now. He was older than her, although not so much so that it turned her off. He was just over forty, still had all of his hair and still had a firmness to his midsection. He exuded strength—not just strength of character, but real, manly strength, the kind she admired. Yes, a man like this, he knew things she did not. He had been around more, had a worldliness about him that was important in keeping her alerted to the dangers in the world. He could impart that knowledge to the boys. He could be the perfect father figure to B.J. and Gabe. It would be a blessing to her for them to grow up and be like Del Mobley someday.

*Pastors,* she thought. *Pastors have to be above the fray. They're held to a higher standard than other men. They preach against things like adultery. I would never have to worry that he would cheat on me or make me a fool.*

*This man is the ultimate catch,* Connie Jo began to think. *It's just like Exa said. She said that a man like this came along once in a lifetime and if I didn't act now, I would never find another like him. Exa was right. This man is perfect in every way. God sent him to me.*

"So, will you marry me? Marry me, Connie Jo. Marry me."

"Yes," she replied. "Yes, I will."

# Chapter Nine

Connie Jo awoke still in her clothes, still on the floor of Vardemen and Exa Shirey's living room. The sun shone in on her, a sobering beacon spotlighting her condition. Next to her was Del Mobley, as if she had never gone to sleep, as if a moment had not passed although it was obviously hours later. He loomed over her, still propped up on his elbow, still staring down at her with his face full of love and affection.

"Del, why didn't you take me home?" Connie Jo straightened herself up and arose from the floor, embarrassed and uncomfortable. "I don't feel good about being here with you. We're not married or anything."

"But we're gonna be—very soon. C'mon, let's tell Cousin Exa and Vardemen." Del took her hand and began leading her into the kitchen.

It seemed like a dream. It had all happened so soon and without any warning. He'd asked her to marry him last night. It was real because there it was, the morning, and he was still talking about it. Now, he was pulling her into the Shireys' kitchen and announcing it while she stood there embarrassed, feeling like something the cat had dragged in, having slept in her clothes on the floor all night long.

"Del, I want to talk to my boys and to my family. I want to meet with them privately to discuss all this with them. I know I said 'yes' last night, but before you go taking ads out in the local paper, I want to talk it out with my people," Connie Jo said.

"Yes, yes, I know, we have to tell the boys. But you don't need anyone else's permission. You're a grown woman with a family of her own. It's not up to your ma and pa or your sisters and brothers. I'm sure they don't run everything by you for your permission, now do they?"

Del was giddy with excitement and Connie Jo hated to be a downer, but it was all too much too soon. She couldn't get her wits about her. Yes, she loved him; she loved Del Mobley. But she loved lots of things—willow trees and puppies and sunsets. She would have liked to have gone on loving him longer, getting to know him more, before deciding she wanted to take this gigantic leap.

She'd never made any major decisions without her family. They were close—closer than close. She even had a twin sister, and twins have a bond that is more unique than regular family. Hers was not a big, overly analytical family, but they kept no secrets. If you took one on, you took on them all.

Del showered up then drove Connie Jo home, where she did the same. She wished he would just leave her alone for a little while, allow her some space so she could inventory her thoughts and feelings, perhaps call one of her sisters or her brother, Rusty, a preacher himself, who had a church up in Colorado now. Rusty was the rock of the family, the person even their parents often went to for support and advice. Rusty would know how to give her guidance. But Del wouldn't leave her alone.

"C'mon, let's take the kids out for a day at the toy store. They look like they haven't had any new things in a while. My treat," he said.

And so off they went. Neither Del nor Connie Jo had said anything yet to the boys, but Del had made a grandiose announcement to Vardemen and Exa Shirey. Neither was what one might term a gossip, but Connie was sure that word would begin to get around, since she had not had the heart to ask them for their discretion.

Children are often simple creatures. B.J. and Gabe, ages seven and five, were ecstatic to go on an adventure with their mother and Brother Del, whom they did not know all that well but had met on a couple of occasions briefly. In downtown Montgomery, Del lavished them with walkie-talkies and toy guns, finishing it all off with ice cream. He was buying them—buying their love and affection. Connie Jo tried to push the cynicism out of her mind, but that was exactly what it looked like. He practically ignored her, but instead played birthday-party clown to the two boys. and they were eating it up. Children of that age have yet to develop cynicism.

*Why was he doing this? Why the rapidity, followed by this big selling job on B.J. on Gabe?* Connie Jo's head spun 'round and ' round. *He's a good man. He's a catch. I've been married before and so has he. Maybe this is the way it goes the second time around. Maybe you don't go through the long months and years of courtship. Maybe you just meet someone who feels right and you pull the trigger, you make the decision and you move on with the next chapter of your life.*

That was the part that Connie Jo could not force herself into: the moving on part. She remained in mourning. She knew it wasn't right. Heck, everyone she knew lectured her about it. But this man, this Del Mobley character, he was doing more than lecturing her. He was making it so. He was planning and plotting out her entire future for her and this was the part she had trouble connecting with.

B.J. and Gabe laughed and smiled. This was as happy as she had ever seen them. Everything they wanted, they got. Even things they would not have dared to be so bold as to ask for—there was Del Mobley, handing them to them, then tousling their hair for good measure. Never before had Connie Jo seen such a charmer.

"Boys, how would you like to have a daddy?" Neither B.J. nor Gabriel made a sound. The question was too oblique, too complex for their little heads. "How would you like *me* to be your daddy?" This they responded to with wild, screeching enthusiasm, as if they'd been asked if they wanted to move to the North Pole to spend the rest of their lives in Santa's workshop, having every toy in the world at their fingertips. What child could refuse?

"Mommy, we're going to have a daddy! Oh boy!"

Connie Jo's heart broke a little. They meant to say, "A new daddy," but that's not how it came out. The boys were already starting to get over Ben Filer. It had been over a year and to a child of five or seven, that's like a lifetime. Suddenly, a daddy sounded like a pony or a BB gun. All the cool kids had one and so they wanted one, too.

Del smiled at Connie Jo, exposing all of his pearly, white teeth. For a moment, she couldn't tell if he was laughing *at* her or *with* them. Her indecision had been beaten. Del had won. He knew what he wanted and Connie Jo did not.

*Maybe he's right. In fact, I'm sure he's right. The boys do need a father and now they'll have one. Not only that, but they'll have a preacher for a father, a good man who will teach them how to walk the straight and narrow. We all have been blessed.*

## Chapter Ten

For the next few days, Connie Jo Filer spent every waking minute with Del Mobley. Between Exa's house, her own house, and being out and about, Del was there from the moment she awoke to the minute she drifted off to sleep at night. She enjoyed the attention, indeed she did, but she had never had such an intense relationship in her life, not even with Ben. He had gone off to do his thing, to go to work, but Del Mobley came to explain that he was "between churches" at the moment, but "there were several interesting irons in the fire" regarding his future ministry.

This did not raise much of an eyebrow with Connie Jo, particularly when Exa Shirey chimed in: "Churches can be so political sometimes. You have these boards and these elders and everybody's arguing and all. Pretty soon, the minister can't take it no more and he's out the door. It's like being manager of a professional baseball team or something."

Connie Jo had seen preachers come and go and so she assumed this was the case. What happened after one had left a church she had belonged to, she never quite knew. Former ministers were like that sometimes—out of sight, out of mind.

The only annoying part regarding this never-ending time spent with Del was that she so wanted to chat with her family about their impending nuptials, but Del kept saying, "I don't know why you think that's so important. You're empowering them to run your life for you. I'm sure they'll like me—most people do—but I really don't need to go through this sort of horse trading. I can imagine someone or other asking me to open my mouth so they can probe around at my teeth." He chuckled.

One day, Del finally did take off for a little while on his own, but before Connie Jo could pick up her phone, there was a knock on the door.

"Yes?"

Before her stood a young woman of around college age. She was tall and attractive, but with a bit of an edge to her and a strong, muscular frame. "Are you Connie Jo Filer?"

"Why yes, I am."

"My name is Rae—Rae Mobley."

For a moment, all time stopped as Connie Jo now studied this girl carefully. Definitely young, but not a little schoolgirl. But, young enough that she most certainly could not be some hidden wife of Del Mobley's. He may have been dashing and handsome, but this girl was so young she could have been—

"I think you know my father, Reverend Delbert Mobley?"

Connie Jo's face paled; her jaw grew slack. "Come on in," she said in a voice as faint as a whisper.

She led the girl to the living room sofa and sat down when she did. For her part, the girl looked uncomfortable and a little agitated, but she still seemed glad to be sitting, relaxing. Connie stared at her, not knowing exactly what to say or how to say it. Still, she looked for familial resemblance and yes, it definitely was there.

"I've been hanging around your house for almost three days now. I take naps in my car during the day sometimes, maybe walk around little. Late at night I go back to the Motel 6 out near the highway, then I set my alarm and get here really early, but it seems my daddy's car is already parked out front. I don't think he knows what kind of car I drive, but I sure do know his."

"Why have you been doing that, child?"

"Listen, I don't know you. Maybe you're nice, maybe you're not. I don't know and I don't rightly care. But I came here to say my piece and I knew I'd never get to spit it out if my daddy were here.

"My daddy married my mom about twenty-three years ago. Me, I'm twenty now. Only child. He wasn't around much when I was growing up, mostly just when I was little.

Then he was off all the time. Pretty soon he stopped coming home altogether.

"I'm surprised he ended up with you here. He'd been seeing this other woman he met on the CB radio. She was a singer. They were together for an awful long time.

"He never gave me or my momma much of anything. He was always saying how tough things were. Yeah," she snorted, "like maybe he should have figured out how much harder it was for a single mother and a daughter to get by.

"Anyways, they never really did divorce—until a few weeks ago. That's why I'm here. I thought you ought to know."

Connie Jo sat dumbstruck. She wanted with all her power to lash out and tell this young lady how wrong she was and to get out of her house. But this girl was calm about it all, like she was recounting ancient history, and there was very little in the way of hopped-up anger in her voice, only matter-of-fact disgust for her father.

"Wh-why...How can this be? Del told me his wife had died and he had no children," said Connie Jo.

Rae snickered. "He tells a good story, doesn't he? Look, the reason I'm here is pretty simple. He's been asking my momma for a divorce since who knows when, but she wouldn't give it to him. Furthermore, he had all these 'conditions' to it anyways. A Baptist minister has a hard time being divorced and all. A lot of churches won't hire you. Course, a lot of churches won't hire my daddy, period, but that's another story.

"Anyway, his daddy, my grandfather, passed on about a year ago. My daddy was the sole heir, so he inherited some money. A little while ago he tried to make a deal with my momma. He said that if she granted him a divorce, he'd give her a lump-sum financial settlement. Again, though, it wasn't going to be straight-up easy. She also had to sign some paper saying she was the cause of the whole breakup and that he was a fine man and a good minister…"

Finally, Rae began to show some emotion—disgust and anger.

"So she signs it. No matter how many times he's screwed her over—sorry if that offends you—she's still a sucker for him. Me, I think I got over him long ago. Don't trust him farther than I can throw him.

"What happens? Same thing that always happens with him. He gets his divorce, he gets his little piece of paper, and then he's off, off like the wind. 'Cept this time, I'm not letting him get away with it. I'd heard him say something about his cousin, Exa, so I tracked him down here and heard he was courting around with you.

"Look, I don't mean you no harm, and that's the truth. You haven't done anything to me and I don't know you from Adam. Frankly, I ain't even out for revenge, strange as that may sound. My father's been gone from my life for most *of* my life and I could care less by now. I just want my momma to get what's coming to her and I figured this was the only way to get it. I could go chasing after him, but that's like trying to catch an eel. He always squiggles his way out.

"But you…" She looked squarely at Connie Jo. "You might be in a position to put a different kind of pressure on him. The last thing on Earth he'd want is for me to be here talking to you, so here I am, sitting right in front of you. I could have threatened him with that, but he'd have figured out a way of keeping us apart or maybe having me killed or something—"

"Now wait just a minute here, young lady." Connie Jo finally felt like a slap had just come smack across her face. "I know families and I know some have their troubles, but now on top of everything else, you're sitting here trying to tell me your father's a killer? I don't think a word you said is the truth. You can say what you will about people. You go around calling them killers and such, you're just so far out of line that nothing you say can be taken seriously."

Rae Mobley sat and smirked. "That one finally got to you, huh? Maybe you should ask him how his father died. Man was in perfect health before he was about to marry a nice, elderly woman who would have gotten a nice chunk of his estate. My daddy didn't like that one bit and then suddenly, my granddaddy died right before the wedding."

Connie Jo rose. "I'm going to have to ask you to get out now. Leave my house at once! I'll call the police."

Rae Mobley slowly rose. "There's no need for that; I'll just see myself out. Listen, I'm only here for one thing: my momma. I know you're going to talk to my daddy when he gets back here. When he does, remember, the only thing I want—in fact, I don't want a damn thing for myself—but all I want is for my momma to have what was promised her. You tell him that and you'll never see or hear from me or her ever again. Frankly, we're both glad to be rid of him forever. But not without what he owes her. You tell him that."

# Chapter Eleven

Connie Jo paced like a caged lioness. *Why? Why, Lord, why?* Oh, how she wanted to call her momma, her sister or her brother, Rusty. But how do you tell a story like this? How do you get them to listen to it from end to end, to understand the context from the beginning to this very moment, so that they truly understand how you feel and what is going on? Why, they barely knew she was seeing Del at all, and none of them had ever met him. How was she going to say, "So, after he proposed to me and I said 'yes,' his daughter showed up at my door and told me tales"?

Exa. Exa was her only option. She had to talk to somebody, and frankly, the thought of talking directly to Del seemed to frighten her. That crazy talk about having people killed. Surely this Rae girl must have been deranged or mentally ill or something. Sure, people said things like, "I was so mad I could have killed him" all the time, but not Del Mobley, not Brother Del. Men like Brother Del weren't like other men; that was why they were men of the cloth. They were called by God to lead others, to set examples through their words and by their actions.

But now, the seeds of doubt had been planted in her mind. The Del she was thinking about was not this man whom the woman who called herself "Rae" was speaking of. Couldn't be.

Connie Jo went upstairs and grabbed B.J. and Gabe and tossed them into her car, then drove off to Exa and Vardemen's. Exa greeted her at the door as happily as ever. "Hiya, sweetie. How's my little cousin to be?"

"Boys, why don't you go play in the yard? I'll be out to check on you in a while," Connie Jo said. Her tone was stern and even the ever-ebullient Exa knew something was amiss as she let Connie Jo pass her by as she strode into her house.

"I get a feeling something is bothering you," Exa said, taking a serious tone herself as she sat down upon her overstuffed living room chair with the white-doily armrests over the floral print.

Connie Jo could not bring herself to sit, but instead she stood and paced, arms folded across her chest. She spun out her tale just as it had happened. Exa seemed deflated at first, then agitated, moving toward the edge of her seat, looking for an opening to speak, to interrupt.

"Listen! Vivian Henninger is nothing but a liar and a tramp. Del married her when they both were young. He stayed with her only a short time and she up and left *him*. Wouldn't let him see his own daughter! Took her away from him. And now she's grownup with a mind all poisoned by her momma. Connie Jo, do you think I would bring you into a situation that would do you and your boys harm?"

Connie Jo stopped her pacing for a moment, then vigorously continued as if attempting to burrow a hole in the hardwood floor. "So, is it all a lie? Did this girl show up on my doorstep to tell me nothing but lies, Exa?"

"No, darlin'. Yes, Del was married before—"

"He told me he was a widower!" Connie Jo said.

Exa paused, staring her down somewhat blankly. "Did he really? That would be a lie and I know my cousin, the preacher, don't lie."

Connie Jo thought. "I can't recall. I know he made it sound that way."

"Look," said Exa. "Consider his position. Baptist ministers are allowed to divorce, but it's frowned upon. Good, churchgoing people hold them up to a higher standard. Don't matter that they all go out and get divorced themselves, but a divorced preacher has a hard time getting work. That's followed Del all his adult life, after that mistake he made marrying Vivian. So, he's learned only to speak when spoken to about it, and he keeps his own counsel. He doesn't gossip about Vivian because he's too good a man to do that to a woman—any woman."

Connie Jo slowed her pacing but still looked troubled, staring down at the floor as if it had answers for her.

"You wanna know the rest, Connie Jo? 'Cause I know

that's what's going through your mind, so I'll tell you what I know.

"Del's been out on his own for years and years. All Vivian ever wanted from him was money, but then she'd sabotage every job he'd ever be hired for. I tell you, the woman is crazy. She wants the man's money, but then she hurts him from earning any! Why do you think a preacher as inspiring as Brother Del doesn't have a church of his own? Why, he could fill one of those mega-churches. He could be on TV! But Vivian is like this stone around his neck.

"As for his daddy, yes, he died not that long ago. Like father, like son—some woman latched onto him and wanted everything from him. The man was all Alzheimered out. He didn't know what was going on. Del, God bless him, tried to step in and keep that woman away from my uncle, and he did, long enough for him to die in dignity and for that woman not to have her fingers in his wallet. As for any 'great fortune' the man had, oh please! He died in a nursing home. They took nearly all his money. You know how those places are. He left Del barely enough to bury him decently and maybe left him a little to live off of. You see how Del lives. Does he put on the airs of a rich man?"

"No," said Connie Jo somberly, lost in thought. "So when did he actually get divorced? *Is* he divorced?"

Exa thought for a moment. "Well, some things I can't rightly answer all by my lonesome. Common sense tells me he couldn't go get a marriage license with you if he were still legally married, so he must be divorced. I know Vivian wouldn't give him a divorce for a long time, but I suppose he must have worked something out with her. If I were you, maybe that's where I'd begin the conversation.

"But please, honey, don't beat up the good man so. He's been through a lot. He wanted that marriage to work and he tried—oh, Lord, I know he tried. And he wanted to be a daddy to that girl of his but Vivian wouldn't let him. Now he meets you and all he sees is goodness and grace. And your boys—my, how he loves your boys. He didn't think he would ever have a chance at being a father again and now your boys…I tell you, Connie, this is a match made in heaven. Both of you are getting exactly what you deserve in this world. The Lord is smiling down on both of you."

# Chapter Twelve

Connie Jo and her boys came home and Del was there waiting for them. She took him aside, shooing the boys away again so she could speak to him in private. Unlike when she first had approached Exa, Connie Jo was now sanguine and subdued, almost frightened, scared of offending Del Mobley with what she was about to ask him. Del, for his part, remained calm, yet still looked insulted and exasperated at times as he heard her out. When she finished, he put up his finger, asking for a moment, and then went out to his car. Returning, he handed Connie Jo a document as she sat pensively in her chair.

"Connie, I did just get officially divorced only a short time ago. I'm sorry if I led you to believe otherwise. It's just that I've learned the hard way to protect myself over the years. My whole history with Vivian has been a cruel, cruel thing, and I pray on it every night. I pray for her salvation and I pray that that painful burden be lifted from me in the most honorable way as I serve the Lord.

"Vivian said she would never grant me a divorce so long as I lived. Can you imagine a woman being that hateful, that spiteful, that she would do that to a man? She didn't understand what it was like to be the wife of a preacher. She thought she was going to be marrying one of these guys with the theme parks and the limousines. And furthermore, she didn't think there'd be any responsibilities placed on her. I thought she was a woman of the church, but she wasn't. I was a young fool led astray by love. She cost me many a job.

"I prayed. I prayed to God to help me find a way out of the hell I'd been put through with her and the way she even took away my little girl. When my daddy died, I went to her on bended knee and handed her every cent I inherited. I gave it all to her if only so that she would grant me that divorce and sign a statement telling folks the truth about our relationship. Connie, I wanted more than anything to get a new start in life. I wanted to marry a good, Christian woman like you, help raise your boys, and get myself a church I could call my own without having to look over my shoulder at what devilishness Vivian was cooking up for me next.

"I want you to read this. This here is the truth. When I sat down with Vivian last, I told her I needed this from her, to clear the air for the world to see, before I would give her her thirty pieces of silver. Go on. Read it."

Connie Jo read and read. It backed up each and every one of Del's and Exa's claims. At the bottom, it was signed by Vivian Henninger Mobley and notarized. When Connie Jo finished, she simply looked down in her lap, spent from all the emotion and trauma of the morning. Finally, she said exhaustedly, "Why didn't you tell me all this? Why did you not even say to me that you had a daughter?"

Del, for the first time, got defensive. "Connie, now, I answered that. I never directly lied to you. I never lied to you at all, for that matter. You asked if I had any little ones. Well, was Rae little? Was she?" Del stopped and looked expectantly at Connie Jo, agitated.

"But Del," said Connie Jo, "that was a lie of omission and you know it. You're acting like a double-talking politician."

"Connie, dammit…" Del exploded, but cut himself off and turned away. His face reddened so much in such a short time that Connie Jo was scared. She'd never seen him like this before. Still, Connie Jo remained composed. This was her house and this was not her husband. She stayed resolute.

"Del, I don't like seeing this side of you. Rae was accusing you of very violent, nasty things, talking 'bout killing your father and such."

"Connie," Del said loudly, then realized he was destroying his own defense by acting as agitated as he was. "If ever I had a mean bone in my body, I'd-a killed Vivian, now wouldn't I? But she's still standing, so I guess that throws out that theory.

"Look, this whole thing is about Vivian and the way she is. I thought it was over once I gave her all my daddy's money and she signed this here paper. But now she's sending out Rae to spook you. She's never going to leave me be."

Del's voice trailed off and he kneeled before Connie Jo as she sat in her chair, his eyes welling up with tears. "I…am a good man. I am, and I believe that you know it, Connie Jo. I wish I could make this go away forever, but it seems Vivian will never let me be. I gave her everything I had, but now it seems she still believes there's more. I ain't got nothing. All I've got…all I've got is you."

Tears were now streaming down his face as he wept unashamedly. Connie had never seen a man cry before her like this.

"Vivian is my cross to bear. I believe we all carry something around with us, and this is my burden. And if you'll still have me, this is what I bring to our marriage. But if you love me, you'll stand by me. I gave my heart to you, Connie Jo. I gave it because I believed you were the perfect woman who could take me as I am. I really thought Vivian was gone from my life and you would never have to deal with this. Maybe this is her last bit of vindictiveness. Maybe she thinks our love is so unsteady that she could tell you anything bad about me and you'd believe it. She probably thinks all women are like her—shallow, selfish and without Christ in their hearts. But you, you're better than her. I know it. I know you'll put aside this last salvo from a mean, godless woman and help me, help us *both* begin a new life together in Christ."

He took her hands in his and bowed his forehead on top of them, his shoulders shuddering as he continued to weep. For whatever reason, all Connie Jo could hear was Exa Shirey's voice in her ear, saying words she'd never said to her before, yet the spirit and meaning were pure Exa: *Forgive him! He has laid himself before you, a man undone. He has confessed his sins and he has shared with you his burden. This is what Jesus calls us all to do, to lift up the burden off of those we love. He loves you. He wants to care for you and your children. You will never meet a better man than this. All people have baggage. How much better would any one of us have dealt with a situation such as this? Cleave to him! Be his wife.*

Del Mobley sat in the car, looking like a man being dragged to the electric chair or a tax audit. "Connie Jo, we don't need this. You're no teenager and I sure ain't."

"Del, I can't believe you! I'm a family-type person and this is my family. We're a package deal, just like me and the boys. Now come on in and stop acting like such a baby.

Don't you *want* to know my family?" Connie Jo said, exasperation coming into her voice.

"I'll know 'em fine. I'll know 'em the rest of my life. What's the hurry? We can meet them after the honeymoon," said Del as he unfolded himself slowly from the car.

"After the honeymoon? You mean you didn't even want them at the wedding?"

"Connie Jo, darlin', we're two old folks—"

"Speak for yourself, you old fool!"

"And we're both doing this a second time. I never thought it looked right for people in that situation to make a big to do out of it. And me being a preacher makes it worse. We'd be waving my whole divorce thing around like a flag. How on Earth am I supposed to get a church that way? I just wanted a quick run down the courthouse just to get it over with. I wanted to do it today. Heck, I wanted to do it yesterday!"

As he spoke, he continued to slowly rise out of the car, hoping that at some point he'd get the go ahead to get back into his seat so they could forget the whole thing, but Connie Jo was determined.

"You'll meet my folks and you'll ask my daddy for my hand. I don't care if we're a hundred and I don't care if this was for the fourteenth time." She seemed proud of herself, speaking her mind and standing her ground, just as she had with Ben back in the old days. She hadn't been much like that with Del. He was older. He was a preacher. There were just so many things about Del that made her hold her tongue.

Once inside, Del was his old, charismatic self. He lit up the room, bouncing from sister to sister, brother-in-law to brother-in-law, backslapping and laughing. One would never think that only a few minutes earlier he had to be dragged kicking and screaming to this place. For as ornery as he was once they'd sat in front of Connie Jo's parents' house, he'd been ten times worse back in Montgomery, before they'd left. But again, Connie Jo stood firm. Meeting the family was a deal breaker.

At a certain point during the revelry, Del nodded at Connie Jo as he made a beeline across the room to where her father was sitting. It was time. Mr. Roberts, for his part, stood looking somberly, almost as if he knew there was more to this visit than simple socializing. Connie Jo watched with nervous trepidation as Del led him into a room off the living room.

Once he got him alone, Del kept up his gregarious ways, but lowered his voice ever so much. "Mr. Roberts, I wanted you to know that Connie Jo and I, well, we've been seeing a lot of each other these past few weeks. Matter of fact, most every day. I do believe I love her, in fact I know it. And she says she loves me, too. And those boys, well, they're just the topping on the pie, as I see it."

He stopped a moment, hoping that Farrin Roberts would let him off the hook, play along and understand where he was going with all this. But Farrin would not budge. He stood like Digger O'Dell at a funeral parlor, a hound-dog slack to his jaw and eyes that looked lonesome as the desert.

"What I'm meaning to say is, I would like your permission to marry her." There, he'd said it. Del sized Farrin up and figured he was a straight-up man who wasn't going to go for his buck-and-shuffle act, and so he stopped it dead cold.

The silence was deadly. Del stood there like a comedian facing a forest of dead trees, a big smile on his face and no reaction from the audience. Finally, Farrin Roberts spoke. "Sir, I love my daughter and what I have to say, I say out of love. Brother Mobley, you have not known my daughter very long, nor she you. I have her to think about and I have my grandchildren to think about as well."

"Well, so do I, on that we agree." Del continued to smile, doing everything but breaking into a tap dance in order to turn Farrin Roberts' frown into a smile, but he was getting nowhere fast. "We both prayed on this, that I can tell you. We both feel good about it."

"Well, son, I'm glad you both feel good," Farrin paused for good measure, "but I sure don't. You may walk out of here thinking it's personal, but it's not. I don't know you well enough for it to be personal, and that's about the whole point I'm trying to make here. You two take some time and then we'll talk." Farrin might have thought for a second that might have been the end to it, but it was not.

"Sir, no disrespect, but Connie Jo and me, we're both of age. We can make our own decisions. What I'm doing here is out of respect."

Farrin looked down at the floor, then back up at Del

Mobley. "Well then, you'll respect my answer. Take some time. Give my daughter a chance to get to know you better. Make sure she knows for sure she can trust you. Marriage, you see, is all about trust. That's what it is at the end of the day."

"Mr. Roberts," said Del, "with all due respect, if you can't trust a minister, who can you trust?"

# Chapter Thirteen

It was a melancholy wedding, made so by Connie Jo Roberts Filer Mobley's family all looking more as if they were attending a funeral viewing than a celebration of newfound and committed love. As for Del, he brought not a single wedding guest—no family, no friends with the exception of Vardemen, who presided, and Exa—odd for a man so charismatic. Connie Jo figured a man like Del Mobley would have a thousand friends.

The engagement had been less than half the time of the courtship, and the courtship could be measured in weeks, not even months. Never before in her life had Connie Jo seen a man so quick to get to the altar, as it were, for they were married discretely in the home of Connie Jo's twin sister, Kelly Sue.

As rapidly as Del wanted to get their relationship legalized, he was equally as anxious about their marriage being known as being so new. That and the letter from Vivian, which he seemed to carry a copy of in the pocket of his pants or sports jacket everywhere he went.

For the life of her, Connie Jo could not understand why every member of her family had such negative feelings toward her nuptials, and by extension, toward Del. Didn't they see what she saw? What Exa saw? What every man, woman and child at the revival meeting in Montgomery had seen? Del Mobley wasn't just a man; he was a superstar, one of those special people God placed upon this Earth to inspire awe in other mere mortals. Del was Billy Graham, Martin Luther King, Jr., Elvis and Richard Petty all rolled up into one. Any fool could see that.

"I don't want to see you hurt again" was what Kelly Sue had said to her. "You've been through so much."

All her people had said some variation on that theme, but what were they thinking? She was still hurting from what had happened to her Ben. She felt it every morning when she woke up and saw Ben's beautiful boys. When she looked in their faces, she saw Ben. So long as they were alive, Ben would always be with her, which was both the best and the worst thing in the world.

And because of that, because she had been through so much, she now realized that the only way to move on was to move on. The bad never really was going to go away, so all that was within her power was to try to push some of it to the side by replacing it with some good, and a good man like Del was exactly what might accomplish that. It was logical, and that was what infuriated her. Her own family questioned her logic, but it was for logic's sake that she was standing there that day, holding the hand of Del Mobley, pledging him her undying love 'til death did they part.

But they were all there—at least, all except Rusty, who could not make arrangements to come down from Colorado on such short notice. That was what Connie Jo felt the worst about. "Del, why can't we wait just another month or two so that Rusty can rearrange his schedule? He means so much to me. He's my rock, even more than my daddy. I can tell Rusty things I can't always bring myself to say to my dad. And I so want you to meet him. He's a minister, too. You two would get along so well. When I'm with you, all I think is, *I wish Rusty were here.* I wish he were with us so he could get to know you and see what I see when I'm with you. Rusty would be your best friend in the world, I'm sure of it."

"I know, and I appreciate what you're saying," Del said. "I want to meet him, too. We preachers got to stick together. We need each other from time to time. Don't worry—maybe once we make this legal and all, we can go on up to visit him. I ain't never been to Colorado. Sounds like it could be a nice vacation for us and the boys."

After the small ceremony, Vardemen Shirey leaned over to Connie Jo and said, "When you two get back from wherever, I'm going to hire Del. I'll put him on staff as educational director if he wants it."

Connie Jo was so excited and so in search of happiness

to grasp on to on this misfit of a day that she quickly ran up to Del and shared with him the good news. But Del's demeanor shifted negatively. "The only reasons why he wants to hire me is so he can have you around and keep an eye out for me."

It was so out of the blue, so incongruent, that Connie Jo didn't know what to say. It sounded jealous and it sounded paranoid—neither of which seemed right, being that it was being directed at Vardemen Shirey, who had helped bring the two of them together, for heaven's sake.

"We could use the job, Del," said Connie Jo.

This, too, Del took like a man who'd just been slapped in the face, although he said not a word. Money had been on Connie Jo's mind over the last few days leading up to the wedding. Her folks had spent as much as they could on her wedding to Ben Filer, but to this affair they contributed little to nothing, although in all honesty, this soiree was not much in need of it; it was no larger than a Thanksgiving dinner with extended family, held in her sister's home.

But money for a small wedding wasn't what nagged at Connie Jo's brain. She had money in the bank and was glad for the security for it. She worked at the church because it kept her whole and had kept her sane during her bluest periods after Ben's untimely death. The money it paid was a pittance and was practically irrelevant. Frankly, Exa and Vardemen nearly had to force it on her, telling her, "Honey, if we don't pay you, the elders will complain because you're keeping a job from another parishioner who needs the money. It's already in the budget."

But while Del never seemed to talk much about money, he also spent very little and Connie Jo had yet to know much about his personal finances. He said he'd given everything he had to Vivian in order to settle his divorce, and yet when he wanted to lavish things on B.J. and Gabe, he did so with impunity and a lack of restraint. He claimed to be helping out part time at a church in LaGrange, Georgia, but he said that only paid about $75 a week and he'd drifted away from it over the past few weeks.

How were they to live? Connie Jo felt that she had enough in savings for her and the boys, but not for a full-grown man who'd want things, big things like a new car and gas to fill it, clothes and what have you. They would need some additional income so that the inheritance from Ben wouldn't dry up by the time they got old.

The wedding was on a Saturday afternoon. Connie Jo and Del's plan was to celebrate with the folks who came and then head out to LaGrange and spend their wedding night in a motel. The next morning, Del would give his last sermon, and then they would head down the coast for a few days of honeymooning.

On the drive to LaGrange, Del was quiet—too quiet. It was odd, this being his wedding day and all. Checking into the motel in LaGrange, there was no passion, no anticipation, and this from the man who had been all hands and lips, attacking Connie Jo like a ravenous animal every time they were alone. But not this day, now that it was welcomed.

"Del, what's wrong?" asked Connie Jo.

He squeezed his lips together as if attempting to close

off the deluge that was about to spring forth. "I'm tired of your family not supporting us in our marriage," he said finally.

"What do you mean, 'supporting'?" she asked.

"I mean approving of our marriage. I'm not marrying your family and your friends. I'm marrying you," he replied.

"Del, my family and my friends love you just as much as they love me."

Del snorted. "That's a lie. They have not made me feel welcome at all."

Connie Jo began to get upset. "Del, it was just that we didn't date but three or four weeks before we got married. They were doing it out of love for me and concern for me. They didn't want you to make a mistake and they didn't want me to make a mistake."

Del continued to unpack and loosen his clothing, adamantly avoiding looking at Connie Jo. "Let's get it straight right now. I didn't marry your damn family or your damn friends, and I don't give a damn what any of them think of me or what they have to say about anything regarding me."

Connie Jo looked at Del as if he were a complete stranger who bore no relationship to the man she had heard preach at a revival barely a month earlier. When he continued to freeze her out, turning his back on her, she began to cry, and once it began, it only continued on and on and on. After about ten minutes, he finally looked her way, but only to say, "Shut up" as he turned over and went to bed.

Later on, she finally contained herself enough to slip under the covers next to him, long after he had already drifted off to sleep.

# Chapter Fourteen

The next morning, Del got up about around eight o'clock and pulled Connie Jo towards him. "Baby, I'm sorry. I'm sorry 'bout what I said last night. I love you." Still, for as much as this was the Del Connie Jo had wanted, the night before had left her feeling emotionally bruised and mentally bewildered.

He stroked her shoulders and reached over to her belly. "C'mon, this is going to make you feel better." He pulled her over to him and starting making love to her, all the while apologizing. But he was not a gentle lover, as a man should be his first time with a woman. To Connie Jo, it almost seemed like despite his words of apology and love, he was actually trying to hurt her, to physically bully her throughout the act.

"Del, not so rough," she eked out. This had the opposite affect, as he continued on rougher and rougher still. "Please, Del, please don't do that." But it was no use. Del Mobley was in a world of his own, alone without her despite their being conjoined. Connie Jo was afraid that he would see her tears, and so she cried on the inside.

When he was through, he said, "Well, did that make you feel better?"

She looked at him with vacant eyes and said, "Yes" in a torn-apart monotone. She was dead inside, damaged inside, scared that if she told him how she really felt, he would only inflict more pain upon her in some way.

This was not the man she had agreed to marry. This was everything that her family had warned her about without specificity. She'd thought she knew him, but this man was someone she did not know at all and she was both frightened and embarrassed because all she thought was how everyone else could see what she could not. If they could see her now, they would have every right in the world to laugh at her dilemma.

Over breakfast, Connie Jo tried to make some sort of conversation as she stabbed unenthusiastically at her eggs. "When we get back, are you going to take that job with Vardemen?"

"Dunno. I'll think about it," he said, staring at the shapely waitress as she leaned over to pour coffee for the table next to them.

Connie caught him looking. "Hey there! Your new wife is over here!" she said playfully.

The glare she got from him would have turned a body to stone. "Don't you ever tell me what to do. I do as I please. I answer to God and I sleep well at night."

"Del, I was just teasing—"

"You'd do better just to keep your mouth shut. You don't be calling me on things. Like I told you, my behavior is between me and God and He ain't complaining and neither should you."

The rest of their honeymoon was either uneventful or full of events similar to their wedding night and the morning after. As for the "for better or worse" aspect of things, Connie Jo viewed things as far more worse than better, much to her chagrin.

*Maybe this is how things are when two people don't know each other all that well and suddenly they're married. They try to stake out their territory, establish their own rules. Besides, he's old enough that he knows who he is and how he likes things,* she thought. Hadn't she and Ben gone through their rough patches, too?

The marking of territory continued when they returned home. Del owned no house—frankly, Connie Jo had never seen where he'd lived prior to their getting married—and so he moved into hers. Whereas some people in such a position might take some time before they feel fully comfortable, Del presented himself as more concerned with what he believed were the traditional roles of men and women in a marriage, regardless of what each had actually brought to it.

In a short time, he was dragging her down to the bank to have all their accounts made into joint accounts. This is normal within a marriage except for one small but important detail: These were Connie Jo's accounts and Del Mobley put not a cent into any of them. As for his accounts, if he even had accounts, they were never even discussed. Still, the mantra was, "We're married now. This is what married people do," and in that instance, he was right…after a fashion.

What seemed less right was how as soon as the new checks arrived, Del took hold of the check registry and disappeared with it. During her marriage to Ben, Connie Jo had always managed the household finances and she, of course, had continued to do so on her own, and so it was less an issue of distrust than of habit and pride when she balked at this.

Del replied, "Baby, I love you more than life itself and I would never take anything from you or the children. If I write a check, you will know it and you will know what it's for. Baby, you have to trust me."

Truth be told, there seemed to be no sneakiness to Del Mobley's financial actions.

"We need new furniture. I look at this place, all I see is another man's home. We need it to feel like it's ours."

"Del, the furniture is only a year or two old. It's practically new, not a thing wrong with it."

Del rolled his eyes. "I told you, it has nothing to do with

the style or quality of the furniture. It's what it represents. Am I your new husband or ain't I?"

And so it came to be. It required more money than was in her—*their*—checking account, so Del managed to also convince Connie Jo to cash in a $10,000 CD. While they were at the bank doing that, he insisted on getting his name put on all her other CDs as well.

Again, she balked. Again, he insisted. Del got out the Bible and said, "This is what Christ requires of me and He requires it of you. Ephesians five, twenty-two, twenty-five: Wives, submit yourselves unto your husbands as unto the Lord, for the husband is the head of the wife even as Christ is the head of the church and He is the savior of the body. Therefore, if the church is subject unto Christ, so let the wives be to their own husbands in everything. Husbands, love your wives even as Christ also loved the church and gave himself for it."

When he finished reading the scripture, he asked Connie Jo if she believed in the Bible. "Of course I do. You know that, Del. I was raised in a Christian home and have been in church all my life."

"Well, this is how I feel about us," he said. "I would give my life for you just as Christ gave His. If you love me as much as I think you do, then you will not question me. You will trust me. After all, that's what love is all about."

The old furniture left, and next to go was Connie Jo's brand-new car.

"It's a girly car. I need a man's car. I'm selling it and

buying a new truck. You can't carry anything in that little car of yours."

Again, she protested. Again, Del whipped out his Bible. Again, Del won the day.

Furthermore, Del commandeered that truck, making it his own, leaving Connie Jo ostensibly with nothing to drive, as they only had one vehicle now between them—Del also had traded in his ragtag, broken-down station wagon that was worthless to begin with.

Soon, all that remained without Del Mobley's name on it were the CDs and the bank accounts in the name of Ben Filer's two boys. For this, Del had a different tactic: "If anything ever happens, Connie Jo, you know the boys will need to be taken care of with it instead of letting somebody else get their hands on it." It seemed wrong, it sounded wrong, it defied logic, considering how much family Connie Jo had, and yet still she succumbed to his charms, for yes, Del Mobley still had his charm.

After another trip to the bank, they went out for lunch together. Sitting across from her, Del just kept staring at Connie Jo, staring and staring, not saying a word, but looking as if he were studying her in silence. Connie Jo felt it best not to interrupt his deep thoughts. Finally, he said, "You are beautiful. I just thank God for giving me a beautiful and wonderful wife."

She took his hand and held it a few minutes before saying how she thanked God for him, too.

Returning home, she found three roses in a bud vase

he had hidden from her, knowing she would come upon it when she cleaned. Attached to it was a card that said, "To the love of my life forever."

That evening, Del played with the boys, something he rarely if ever did. He got their storybooks down and read to them as they sat on his lap. When he put them into bed, he said to them, "Daddy loves you and Mommy loves you."

Daddy. That was what he wanted them to call him, and for as much as that tugged at Connie Jo, seeing it in this context made her glow. Daddy. Her boys had a daddy again and they liked it, because he acted like a daddy and loved them like a daddy, and wasn't that what the boys wanted and needed?

In bed, Del was loving and compassionate that night—very, very tender. It was by far the best night of their three-week-old marriage. *This is going to work,* dreamed Connie Jo. *This is going to work.*

# Chapter Fifteen

Vardemen Shirey's job offer to Del Mobley sat on the table, so to speak, for over two months. During that time, Brother Del did not work a lick, but stayed at home and tagged along on all of Connie Jo's errands and activities. Not that he appeared enthusiastic about what she did; it almost seemed to her as if he felt he was her guard dog, her protector.

"Del, I can go to the grocery store by myself. I've done it my entire life." But still, he tagged along. His excuses were weak, but he delivered them with such authority and determination that it seemed that the man became set in whatever ways he declared, for whatever reason that made sense to him and only to him.

Del's boredom progressed into entertaining himself

by making purchase after purchase—a camera here, new fishing equipment there. All top-of-the-line stuff, all with Ben Filer's money. For this, he seemed to feel no shame or remorse. "What's mine is yours and what's yours is mine," he would say, excepting the fact that Connie Jo had yet to see what exactly it was that was his and not truly hers to begin with.

Vardemen pressed and pressed, perhaps out of the sincere feeling that having Del Mobley on his staff would be a feather in his cap, or simply because he didn't like the way his wife's cousin was just lazing around, sponging off of one of his parishioners. Finally, Del reluctantly accepted the job offer. "It's beneath me, Connie Jo. Why, I can preach rings around that stiff. He just wants me under his thumb so he can feel he's superior to me. Well, I'll show him. I'll take his piddly little job just to spite him."

And thus it began. Around Vardemen and Exa, Del Mobley was all laughs and positive energy. But when he arrived home from working at the church, he looked like an angry bulldog, his cheeks all puffed out as if he'd just been in a fight and was looking for another. Connie began to dread Del's coming home.

"Why on Earth do you feel this way? Do God's work and then who knows? We can do anything you'd like. You can apply for a church anywhere you want. Del, I just want you to be happy. I want us all to be happy. These should be the good times."

To assuage his anger, Del would simply come home with

another expensive toy every week or so. A new watch, a new suit. On occasion, it would be something for Connie Jo or the boys—one day, a pair of diamond stud earrings for her. They took Connie Jo's breath away, yet later on the reality hit her: She had paid for them herself. She still worked at the church and she knew what Del was being paid, and it wasn't enough to afford these sorts of luxuries. But it was the only thing that kept him placated.

A pastor receives invitations from parishioners to visit and break bread with them. It was the sort of thing Connie Jo enjoyed, for she was almost always invited to join Del. But it occurred to her that some invitations Del was passing off and avoiding, while with others he was Johnny on the spot. Because of the temper he'd been showing, she didn't dare confront him and question him, but after a time she began to notice a pattern: If a family was active, wealthy or influential in the church, he supped with them readily. If they were not, he slithered away.

He was networking. Connie knew the score. Her Ben had had to do some of the same as an engineer, kissing up to all the right people even if he didn't care to deep down. But Del was a minister. Ministers weren't supposed to be so transparently shallow and personally ambitious. Besides, there wasn't any merit pay involved in this job. And as for opportunity for advancement, there was only his job—and Vardemen's.

Over the next few months, Del seemed to work less and less. When confronted, he would tell Connie Jo that he was out of the office, making face-to-face calls and doing survey work, not staying stuck behind a desk. "Vardemen is making me do all the scut work while he sits on his butt and takes all the credit and glory for everything. The only good thing he does is socialize with the parishioners. I think I'm going to go before the board of deacons about it."

"Del! That man helped introduce us, and he gave both you and me jobs. Why would you back bite him so? He's done every good thing a Christian man should do."

Del put on his bulldog look. "Yeah, and his magic certainly seems to be working on you. Why do you think I'm around here as much as I am? I figure someday, I'll open up the door and he'll be in here with you, all alone, just the two of you. I know what men see when they look at you."

"Del, that's crazy talk! Vardemen is family now, and he's the most honest, decent man I know."

"The *most* honest? The *most* decent? You really mean that? And what about me?" Del growled.

"Oh, stop this nonsense now. For the love of Jesus, this is insanity," Connie Jo cried.

Del Mobley could pull off a silent treatment as well as any man or woman. He'd done it a number of times during their short marriage, and he appeared ready to do it again. He brushed past Connie Jo and headed toward the stairs to their bedroom. Connie Jo gave chase, trying to clarify herself and make peace with her man. When she got about halfway up the stairs behind him, he turned, took his foot, and kicked her back down to the bottom.

When Connie Jo hit the floor at the base of the stairs, she was knocked unconscious. When she came to, Del had his arms around her as he asked, "Are you alright?"

"I don't know. I don't think so," she replied through the pain. As she tried to sit up, she felt a terrible pain on her left side. "I think I broke some ribs. My head hurts. I think I'm going to throw up. Please, Del, call me an ambulance. I think I should get looked at. I ought to get X-rayed."

"Oh, darlin', all you need is some tender loving care from your husband."

"No, Del," she said adamantly, "I need to see a doctor. Take me to the emergency room."

This went back and forth and back and forth, yet Del was insistent that Connie Jo did not need medical attention and furthermore, he was not going to accommodate her in receiving any. Being that she was hurting too much to do much about it on her own, she wilted a little, giving herself up to inevitability. It didn't take a genius to figure out where Del was coming from.

*If we go to the hospital, they'll ask what happened and he's afraid I'll implicate him in kicking me down the stairs. He'll get in trouble and never work again as a minister. For that reason, he'd sooner I die or never heal right. Fine, then. I'll put my life in the hands of God and hope for the best. His will be done,* she thought.

Del picked her up and put her on the floor in front of the fireplace.

"Del, I appreciate your moving me, but put me on the

couch or in bed. I don't want to be lying on the hard floor. It hurts."

Del Mobley loomed over her. "*You* know what you need. You just won't admit it." It was an odd thing to say, and it was totally inappropriate that he was saying it so lasciviously. He should have been begging for mercy, apologizing to high heaven, extolling her to forgive him for hurting her so, for there was no mistaking that this was all his fault, whether he truly meant to hurt her or not. Yet his mind now went in a wild direction.

"Del, if you're not going to let me see a doctor, the only thing I want is to be made comfortable and left alone."

Del Mobley began to take his clothes off, saying, "No, this is what you need." He began to undress her.

Connie Jo protested. "Del, please don't! You've already hurt me. I'm not able to have sex with you. Not now. Please leave me alone."

But still, he kept on undeterred.

"Del, you're sick! You are sick. You need help. For you to treat me like this in the shape I'm in…Del, there's something wrong with you! Get off of me. Get me off the floor!"

He didn't do anything as far as helping her get up until after he had gotten what he wanted and was finished with her. When he was through, he said, "I know that made you feel better," and he meant it. The look on his face clearly indicated that he believed that what he had just done, pistoning on top of a physically broken woman, was a gift he had given her, a balm for all that ailed her.

"No," she said through her tears. "No, it didn't. I was in nothing but pain and you knew it. I know you knew it because I kept telling you so and any fool could have figured it out even if I were a mute."

Still, Del Mobley acted as if he had not heard of word of this, confidently redressing himself, looking full of pride and swagger.

"Just stay away from me, now," Connie Jo said. "I'm gonna crawl up into bed and take some aspirin. I'm hurting so bad."

# Chapter Sixteen

Day after day, Del became more and more of a fixture around the house—odd for a man who allegedly had a full-time job. It seemed as though he never worked past lunchtime; every day he wandered up their walkway around noon, looking for a bite to eat, and never returned to his endeavors.

"Del, aren't you going back to work?" Connie Jo asked. It had been a week after the incident on the stairs and she'd said very little to him, but remained in fear of angering him again as she had that fateful day. She'd suffered a concussion and broken ribs. She knew the head injury was from the initial fall to the floor, but she wondered how much worse her ribs were from Del hopping on top of her and forcing himself upon her, virtually raping his own wife when she was in a condition where she had no chance of fighting him off.

She could not for the life of her figure out what had gone on in his head that day, how he could have ignored her pleas. He had to have heard her. It must have pleased him. *What sort of man would find pleasure in raping an injured woman?* she wondered. *What kind of man is my husband?*

"No, I'm done for the day," Del answered. "Vardemen told me I could have the rest of the day off to spend time with my lovely wife."

Some days Del would just lounge around, not doing much of anything, while other days he would cook up some fun adventure such as a ride into the country or a shopping trip. But Connie Jo had trouble separating the man who had raped her from the man who spent time with her now and still shared her bed. She also couldn't understand why Vardemen Shirey would hire Del at a full-time salary to only work a few hours a day.

The phone rang and Connie Jo answered it. "Connie, this is Vardemen. Is Del there?"

"Why yes he is."

"May I talk to him?"

Connie alerted Del, who asked that she hang up the kitchen phone while he picked up in the den. She did so and continued about her chores, but without even attempting to listen in, she could not help but hear Del's voice become louder and louder the longer he stayed on the phone with Vardemen. When they finished, Del came back into the kitchen wearing his angry bulldog face, the same one he'd worn the day he'd injured her.

"Is everything alright?" she asked meekly, not wanting another go-around like they'd had the week before.

"Fine," he spit out before settling back in and allowing the red to flush out of his face. "He and Exa wanted us over for dinner tonight but I said you were already cooking."

"Oh, I don't mind. We haven't eaten with Vardemen and Exa for ages. We used to get together all the time. Why don't you call him back and invite them over here?" Connie Jo asked daintily. She knew Del was lying, but she didn't want to call him on it directly.

"Naw, Exa's in the middle of cooking, too. That wouldn't work at all," Del harrumphed.

---

The next morning, around ten-thirty, Vardemen Shirey was knocking on Connie Jo's door. "Is Del here?" he asked.

"Why, no," Connie Jo replied. "He went to work. I thought he'd be at the church with you."

"Connie Jo, may I wait on him here?" Vardemen asked.

"Of course, come on in," she replied. As Vardemen made himself at home, Connie Jo noticed the look of discomfort on his face. "Vardemen, is anything wrong?"

Vardemen visibly winced. "Yes, there's a lot wrong with Del. He's not doing his job. He's trying to cause friction between the church members and I won't tolerate that among my staff. If we can't work together in peace, then we don't need to work together at all."

Connie Jo sat across from Vardemen at her dining-room table. "Vardemen, Del says you've been sending him home early every day, giving him lots of time off."

Vardemen Shirey rubbed his chin, then looked straight at Connie Jo. "Connie Jo, what do you think of that? You still work part time for me. Does that make any sense to you?" He did not wait for an answer. "Del is not the man I thought I knew. I got sold the same bill of goods you did by Exa. Now, she's my wife and I'd never speak ill of her and I do not suspect her of being anything less than forthright, but I think she's been snookered, too. She and Del are cousins and all, but they've not always been that close, so there are a lot of gaps in what she seems to know and what she doesn't about who he is and how he's lived his life since they've grown up and moved along."

Automatically, Connie Jo began to defend Del. "But he's good. He's of God."

"Connie, not everybody is of God," Vardemen replied.

"Are you trying to tell me something? Do you know something about him I need to know?" Connie Jo asked.

Vardemen became contemplative. "I can't rightly say I know much of anything I didn't already know going into this whole thing. I do know I always had a gut feeling about certain things, but I held my tongue because he's family. I never liked his style, but I tried to rise above that. But the way he's gone about his work, how he's slacked off, not doing what he's getting paid for, turning this one against that one…"

Just at that moment, Del Mobley pulled up in his new truck, and Connie Jo got excited and nervous. "Vardemen, you shouldn't be here."

"Wh—what? Connie Jo, you invited me in. What's the problem?" he asked.

Connie Jo flitted around, her hands waving through the air like wild sparrows. "Del's here and he's gonna get mad."

"Connie Jo…" Vardemen's voice trailed off and his brow furrowed. "Connie Jo, are you afraid of this man? I'm your pastor. Is he hurting you? You look awful scared."

But before Connie Jo could answer, Del Mobley was in the house, a serious look upon his face. "Vardemen, whatchu doin' here?"

"Looking for you, Del. We need to talk."

Del Mobley hung up his coat. "We got nothing to talk about, Vardemen."

"Oh yes we do, Del," said Vardemen. "We can either talk here or we can go to the church office and talk."

Del Mobley puffed out his chest. Indeed, he was a finer physical specimen than Vardemen Shirey—younger, with a stout upper body and thick arms. But Vardemen Shirey did not back down, nor did he fall into the trap of allowing this to get out of hand. "I'm not leaving my home," said Del. "If you've got something to say, you can say it here."

And so he did. Vardemen Shirey did not raise his voice, nor did Del Mobley swoop in too quickly to quiet him from his soliloquy. He repeated and elaborated upon the charges he had made to Connie Jo as Del's face reddened. "You're spoiled, Del. I don't know what happened to you, but you're going to have to make some changes in your life if you're going to work with me."

Del finally erupted. "What are you going to do, fire me?"

"I was fixing to fire you, but—"

"Well, then, I quit. I quit because I'm not going to have that on my record—that I was fired from a church," said Del.

Vardemen Shirey tipped his head toward the floor, grimaced, and then sardonically half smiled. "Del, you've been fired from several churches. I can understand pride and wanting to put on a show for your little lady, but you also owe her some honesty. She hasn't known you that long and by the look on her face, she hasn't checked up on you the way that I have."

"Vardemen, I'm gonna have to ask you to leave my home," Del exclaimed. "And if we can't work together, we can't socialize together neither." It seemed as if Del Mobley was straining to keep his chest inside his shirt and his fists attached to his arms.

After Vardemen Shirey let himself out, Del Mobley was all over Connie Jo, smacking her in the face with open-handed blows. "I told you never to have another man into our home! You are going to obey me. When I tell you something, you are going to abide by it."

Connie Jo held her arms aloft, trying to block his blows

as best as she could. "Del, what was I going to do? Tell Vardemen he couldn't come into our house? That you didn't trust him? That you're jealous of him?"

"You could have told him to call me," he said. "You should have sent him on his way." And still, the slaps pounded her forearms and the sides of her head.

"Del," she cried, "you can do whatever you want to with me. You know I'm a good person. You know that I'm a good wife. You know in your heart that Vardemen Shirey is a good, Christian man and he would never do anything to harm his ministry or to put shame upon his ministry, and neither would I. If you don't know me well enough by now to know that I'm good and that I'm a faithful wife to you, then we don't need to be married if you can't trust me."

He threw her up against the wall, choking her. "I need a wife who will stand by me. One who won't go against me."

Connie Jo strained to catch her breath, eking out, "Del, I'm not going against you. I've never said anything negative against you to anyone. I just won't do that. I do stand by you. Please, put me down and stop hurting me."

"No, you're just like Vardemen and all the rest of them. You can't see the good side of me. All you see is the bad side." His eyes were wild, unable to see the ludicrousness and insanity of the situation he had created. "I got you figured out just like I figured out Vardemen Shirey. I ain't been put on this here Earth so I can be some other man's nigger." He belted her again for good measure, this time with a closed fist. "And I ain't yours, either."

# Chapter Seventeen

For the next few weeks, Del Mobley sat around the house like a living-room fern, doing little more than collecting dust and requiring nourishment. Connie Jo still went to her part-time job with Vardemen and Exa, but there were strains everywhere, both at home as well as at the church.

"Connie Jo, you know Exa and I hold nothing against you at all. Not a thing. In fact, we apologize to you for…" Vardemen Shirey glanced sheepishly at his usually boisterous wife, who uncharacteristically pursed her lips and remained quiet. "Maybe getting you into a situation that has not been as wonderful as we had all imagined it might be."

Connie Jo's fallback position was always simply to put on a smile and act graciously. "Oh, now, let's all get our sorries out of the way and forget about it. I'm just as sorry. I'm straining to make you all understand how much I love you and how much you've done for me, and I'm also dedicated to being a good wife to Del. He needs me, he does. He comes off so strong and all, but I'm learning that's a lot of show, you know what I mean? I think he's gone through a lot in life and these are the things he does to cover up the pain. He has too much pride because he's afraid of opening up and letting people see how much damage he's sustained."

Exa remained silent and Vardemen simply bowed his head slightly and said, "Connie Jo, you make me humble to be the one they call 'pastor.' You missed your calling, I feel. God bless you."

Back at home, Del was less appreciative. Mostly, he watched TV and ignored her, giving her the silent treatment yet breaking that posture just long enough to toss a verbal hand grenade at her from time to time, usually when she returned from work.

"So, back from seeing your boyfriend?" was a common one. There was no puckish humor to it; Del Mobley meant it in the worst way. After a time, Connie Jo simply ignored it and put on a fake smile for her boys so that they would think everything was alright—and everything *was* all right, for she would make it so. She went about life as their mother just as she had before she'd married the large, potted plant sitting in front of her living-room television set.

Indeed, Del even began to look less and less like a vital man and more like a lump of something to be taken out with the trash. His weight accumulated and his personal care declined. When she wasn't thinking more in terms of making sure the boys were leading as normal lives as possible, she worried if Del was in some serious state of depression. That, of course, was giving him the benefit of the doubt, which she was destined to do, for it was her way.

Occasionally, the boys' lives were far less than normal. Del attempted parenting, but only in the role of enforcer and punisher. One night, Gabe and B.J. were horsing around after lights out. Connie Jo made a move towards their room, but suddenly the cold volcano that had been Del Mobley awoke from his stasis.

"I'll take care of this."

There it was again: the bulldog face, the one he put on when he was mean and vicious, hateful towards the world, and Connie Jo panicked. When Del arrived in the boys' room, he pulled back the covers, popped them on their behinds and told them, "Shut up! Get quiet in here or I'll take my belt to you!"

Connie Jo was quickly at his side. Del's tone was vicious and angry, as if once he'd begun thrashing them he would not know when to stop. "Del, the kids are only kids. You want to put my boys in adult bodies. You want them to act like adults and it's just not right."

Del suddenly reached for a brush that was lying on the dresser and struck Connie Jo on the behind several times. "I guess you want some, too. You shut up and you get yourself back in bed. I'm the man in charge here!"

"Del, you're sick! You need help. I just can't believe that

you jumped on my children for no reason at all and the same with me. Did you do that to your own daughter?"

Connie Jo wanted to reach out to the air to pull back that last phrase. Del Mobley's eyes turned to smoldering slits, his fat cheeks red with anger. He grabbed her by the collar and pushed her up against the wall right there as Gabe and B.J. looked on, terrified and unable to help. He shook her and shouted, "Shut your damn mouth! Don't you *ever* bring up my daughter again. You're just like all the other women. You're stupid." He released her and turned his back on her as she touched herself all around her head and shoulders, making sure she was alright and nothing was bleeding.

"Go to bed now," she whispered to Gabe and B.J. "Don't you be worrying about all this. You made—" She almost said "Daddy," for that was what Del kept forcing them to call him, but this time she could not go along with it. Instead, she simply let the thought go unfinished, her eyes welling up with tears.

*They'd* had *a daddy, and now instead they have this man, and that's all my fault!* she said to herself. *And what does he mean by 'all the other women'?*

Anyone looking in as a silent observer upon her life would instantly assess that Ben Filer had been the far better husband and father than Del Mobley, yet Connie Jo had changed in her role as wife. She actually treated Del superficially better, although she most certainly had loved Ben more, with less reservations in her heart.

But she carried with her the burden of survivor's guilt. Although she'd been millions of miles away, she felt she'd had a hand in his untimely death, and for that she could never quite forgive herself. Her penance was Del Mobley, to dote on him as she wished she had doted on Ben, to put up with Del as she had not with Ben. With Ben, she'd been feisty and stubborn, and so with Del she would be docile and declawed, putting up with and taking whatever it was this man dished out, for this was her punishment from God.

She shared none of this with her family. They knew nothing of Del's physical, mental and emotional abuse, for if they did they would surely rise up as one and kill him or have him arrested. The Robertses were a tightly knit family, and yet, to avoid having to lie any more than she had to, Connie Jo began to speak to them less and less. She felt isolated and yet she was not, for she still attended church regularly, still worked with Exa and Vardemen, still came home to the boys and to Del. Yet only with the boys did she feel the ability to relax somewhat and open up, though not about Del, of course, for they were still, in her eyes, far too young to burden with those troubles.

But at least with her sons she could chat and chatter, something she was less apt to do around Exa, as both women felt a sense of guilt by association—ironically, both due to their association with the same person: Del Mobley.

One day the phone rang at home and it was Rusty, blessed Rusty, her older brother. "Hey, sis, how's it going? I just wanted you to know, I'm making a move. I'm coming back down south. I can't take these crazy Colorado winters anymore—I wasn't raised for that."

Just the sound of Rusty's voice made Connie Jo feel alive again. "I got a new church. I'm coming down to St. Augustine, Florida. We should be there in about a week."

Connie's spirits rose palpably, yet her mind turned to the man perpetually in her living room: Del. She fell silent, depressed once more. Her marriage wasn't working; it wasn't working at all. Del wasn't working at all, and that stood at the heart of it.

"What's the matter, sis? I thought you'd be happy I'm coming closer to y'all. I'll only be 'bout six, seven hours away. That's a heck of a lot better, wouldn't you say?"

"Rusty," she said, "you may have heard, but Del is between ministries right now. The thing here in Montgomery didn't work out. It…it wasn't quite what he was looking for. Del needs his own church, Rusty. Can you do me a favor?"

"Anything, kid. You know you can ask me anything," he replied.

Connie Jo stared right at Del, speaking loudly enough so that he would hear her, yet still afraid of what might set him off, causing him to hurt her again. But she was on the phone with Rusty, and just the sound of Rusty's voice made her feel like she had the strength of legions. "Rusty, once you get settled in, could you see if there's any pulpits empty 'round there?"

"Sure," Rusty said enthusiastically, then cut off the rest of his own sentence in order to collect his thoughts. "Maybe what I should do is come spend some time with you two once I get down there next week. How much of a bind are you two in? I'll be quite busy setting up my ministry, but as soon as I can, I'd like to meet the man—get to know him better."

Connie Jo knew Rusty all too well. The Roberts family knew enough not to tip their hands and say too much when words weren't necessary or prudent. Connie Jo seemed to understand the unspoken message clearly through the phone lines—Rusty, who would have stepped in front of a bullet for his sister, Connie Jo, had heard some negative tales about this Del Mobley character and thus was disinclined to vouch for him sight unseen. Connie Jo respected that, for Rusty was all things good and wise.

"Good," she replied. "We can wait. I've got money in the bank and a part-time job. We'll be okay for a while. I just can't wait to see you. I miss you so. I really want you to meet Del. It'd be great if you two could become friends."

She said this wistfully, as it had been one of her dreams shortly after meeting Del Mobley. Rusty was a preacher and a fine man. Del had seemed the same way, and she had envisioned the two of them standing shoulder to shoulder, spreading God's message. Now she looked at Del as a man fallen from grace. Perhaps Rusty could rescue him from his demons.

# Chapter Eighteen

As promised, Rusty Roberts came over to meet his new brother-in-law, Del Mobley, shortly after he settled in at his new church in St. Augustine. Del spruced up and actually seemed motivated and full of life for the first time in months.

*Maybe this is it,* thought Connie Jo. *He needs to feel needed. He needs to feel the fire inside for his work, for his ministry. This man needs his own church and I shall do whatever it is I can do in order to make that dream a reality.*

Playing hostess, Connie Jo was happier than she'd been since she could not remember, and Del Mobley, playing host, suddenly acted like the gregarious man she'd first met that night at the revival. *This is good,* she thought. *This is right.*

All three—Rusty, Connie Jo and Del—seemed anxious to begin talking in earnest, but none wanted to be the first to speak. At one point, Rusty managed to pull his sister upstairs for a private moment. "Connie Jo, if you are having problems, tell me so I can help you," he said, a worried looked etched across his brow.

"No, Rusty," she said. "We're not having any problems. But if you knew of a church in need of a preacher, that would certainly lift all our spirits. You know how that is."

"So it's nothing more than that?" he asked quizzically.

"No, nothing at all. Things are fine. I love Del. Once you get to know him, you'll love him, too," she said. Her hands and eyelids fluttered, perhaps giving away her obfuscation, but at the heart of it all, what she said was at least partially true. She *had* seen the good side of Del Mobley and knew it to be there. But it seemed like a seed stillborn within the Earth, edging close to the surface but needing something, some nourishment or encouragement, in order to bloom. Maybe Rusty could help.

Once they returned downstairs, the three of them sat down for more serious discussion. Del said all the right things, as if he'd been priming himself, staying three moves ahead of his inquisitor at all times. Finally, Rusty leaned back and said with a sigh, "Well, I did hear of a pulpit that might be available in Gainesville. It's not quite as large a congregation as mine, but perhaps you could come in and do good work there. It'd be all yours—you'd only answer to the board of deacons. Full-time, decent salary. It's probably only about an hour, hour and a half away from me and my family. I know the rest of the family, our parents and our brothers and sisters, would be pleased. It's a bit of a ride out from Alabama to there, but at least Connie Jo and I would both be pretty much together and they'd be more apt to come pay us all a visit more often. What do you think of that, Del?"

Had he not addressed Del specifically, Connie Jo thought she would have jumped out of her seat to scream, "Yes, we'll take it!" But it wasn't her place to do so and so she simply smiled from ear to ear, waiting for Del's answer.

"Well, of course I'm interested."

"I'll let them know and they'll probably schedule a trial sermon with you in a few weeks. If there's anything else you need to know, just give me a call."

Rusty got up to leave, embracing his sister and getting a gracious and vigorous handshake from Del. As he opened the door to leave, he half turned to both of them, fixing a sideways stare at Del. "Just so's you know, I'll be speaking on your behalf. We still don't know each other very well, so I trust my faith is well placed, Brother Del. If God is in it, it should happen. Meanwhile, I suggest you and my sister pray on it and I shall pray on it, too."

With that, he turned and left, not waiting for an answer. It served to let a little air out of the balloon, so to speak, but Rusty had said it in a way that was meant to be professional rather than catty.

Del turned to Connie Jo and again looked like the man

who had swept her off her feet while they were still dating. "Connie, I love you. You're special to me and you're special in the ministry. You're very special to God. You won't be sorry you brought me together with your brother. God is going to bless us." And he hugged her.

Through the warmth of his strong embrace, Connie Jo said, "I know God is with us, Del, and as long as we are doing His work, God will take care of us and God will bless us in every way."

~

"I have one trepidation, Connie Jo—one thing that might stand in the way of my getting that or any other church."

It was the day they were to meet with the board of deacons in Gainesville, and both of them had been fussing around all morning, picking out just the right outfits and going over their stories—what they might be asked and how they should answer. It was stressful and exciting all at the same time.

"What's the matter, Del? What are you worried about?"

"The boys."

"What do you mean? They're fine boys," she answered.

"That ain't the problem. The problem is, when they go to school, they'll carry the name Filer and everyone will ask questions, start rumors."

"Del, I'm a widow. The explanation is plain and simple.

People would look up to you for marrying a widow and her children as you have."

Del Mobley started to pace, wiping his mouth with his hand and immersing himself in his invented dilemma. "The boys should have my name. They're young and we're moving. No one in Gainesville knows them. We wouldn't be lying—I don't want to lie. I got this here piece of paper from Vivien about the divorce. That part's fine unless she up and tries to ruin me again. But every time someone sees the boys, I don't want it to get to some big, long discussion about our private life. That's no one's business but our own. If they took the name Mobley, it would cut that off right there. Besides, I've always wanted to adopt the boys. I *am* their daddy. They *call* me Daddy."

Connie Jo, who was nervous about the events of the day as it was, was not in the best state of mind to form a cogent argument. "Del, this isn't the time. We have to leave for Florida in less than a half hour. I need time to think on this and pray on such a thing. I'd need to talk it over with the boys. I'd want to talk to Ben's folks. They had no other son than Ben. The boys are carrying on their family name. My first inclination is that it wouldn't be right."

Del Mobley quickly turned as if slapped. "I don't have time. This is my big day and you're going to ruin it. You'll ruin everything. If I don't have my mind set at ease, I can't make my case in front of these folks. It may not come up tonight, but it sure as hell will come up on Sunday if they ask me to do a trial sermon. We'll be bringing the kids, and people will ask. No, this is what we're going to do. It's settled. As of tonight, they're *my* boys and their last name is Mobley. As soon as we get back home, we'll go to the lawyer and have it changed legally."

"Del! That's not your decision. The boys have a say. I have a say."

Del loomed over her, his face less than an inch from hers. "No one has a say in this house but God and me. This is a gift I am giving them and you. All I want to hear about it is 'thank you kindly.'"

No sooner did they get into the car than Connie Jo began to weep uncontrollably. Ben's name. All she had left were the boys, each of them bearing Ben's name. Now even that would be gone. She turned her head away so that Del could not see her, for surely if he did he would rail at her and then blame a poor interview on her.

At the first opportunity, she pointed out an upcoming rest stop and asked him to pull over so she could use the bathroom. Once inside, she dabbed at her eyes and reapplied her makeup. Her depression was palpable. She had so looked forward to this day. Del would get this job and he would be Brother Del again, a great man with his own church, and she would be a real preacher's wife and her boys would stand tall and proud. Now she understood that because of Del's controlling ways, it all came at a price: Ben's name, Ben's legacy. She would never be able to face her old in-laws again, for no explanation in the world would sooth them; they would be crushed and insulted to the core.

*Is this the trade, God? In order for this piece of happiness, to do your good works, is this the sacrifice I must make? If so, let it be thy will.* And yet she wondered, as she often did, was it God's will or Del Mobley's? In Del's mind, there was never any difference.

When she returned to the car, she knew she could not keep herself together for the many hours ahead and so she asked if Del minded if she crept into the backseat in order to lay down, so she would be fresh for the interview. He made a catty remark about how much more important it was that he be fresh, but otherwise he let it go.

There, in the backseat, she buried her head underneath her coat and wept as silently as possible, feeling utterly despondent. *Please God, don't always test me like Job. Please, if it is at all possible, let me simply do your work without having to give up everything I hold precious to me on this Earth. I gave up Ben. I've given up so much happiness because of your messenger, Del, and now I must give up Ben's legacy. Please, allow me to give back to you, God, without fear that so much more must go out from me against my will.*

The silent prayer made her feel guilty and shameful, yet even that did not quell her tears.

*I am weak, God. Give me strength.*

—

Sitting in front of the board of deacons was not unlike an inquisition. Del attempted to be the strong, charismatic Brother Del who prowled the altar like a man possessed by God himself, but Connie Jo, who knew him better than anyone else there that day, could see the strain it was all having on him. He perspired and his face was flushed, yet he tried to enthusiastically answer each and every question so perfectly that they could not possibly think to hire anyone else.

When they'd first gotten married, Del had told Connie Jo how important it was for her to look good on his arm. Being a minister's wife meant having to look good all the time, and so, to please him, she worked on it assiduously. Prior to this meeting, he had gone over a list of instructions: Be congenial with the people and act like a first-class pastor's wife.

"You are the first lady. You're the first lady in my life. People will treat you like that if you act like a first-class pastor's wife."

She followed his lead and, in her own way, was, perhaps, doing an even better job than he during the interview, smiling so sincerely that she sparkled, all the while praying silently that she could continue to speak as little as possible. *We need this, Lord. Please let it be your will and I will again turn my entire being up to thee.*

When asked about her, Del flattered her by saying, "Connie Jo and I have a lot in common. The main thing is that we both love the Lord, and we're anxious to do the Lord's work. I love Connie, and I love our boys."

Del said all the right things, but Connie Jo, of course, could now see the exacting way in which he chose all of his words. No talk of second marriages; no mention of B.J. and Gabe not being his natural children. Lies of omission, not commission. It made her nervous and, she surmised, it was what made him even more nervous.

Oh, how she wished he did not feel the need to lie so often. That was the strain that was wearing the man down, she felt. She had tried many times to convince him that churches and churchgoing people were a forgiving sort, but he would have none of it. He would split hairs and sidestep questions he did not want to answer honestly, never believing that he could simply lay his life on the line and still be judged a good man with a talent and a purpose in Christ.

Del mentioned that part of his interest in this church was so Connie Jo could be closer to her brother, Rusty—another lie. Connie Jo's smile began to show cracks. Did it show?

Far more relaxing was the trial sermon he preached three days later. Del roamed the altar, picking at people in the pews and joking in order to make them all feel at ease and to ease his own nervousness, which, when he was in his element, was visibly nonexistent. But when he got down to it, he preached hellfire and brimstone. The church, brimming with nearly 300 people—far more than the parish's usual showing—became as one in the enthrallment of a master preacher possessed by the spirit.

At the end of the service, a deacon asked Brother Del to make an announcement asking the congregants not to leave while quietly whispering that if he and his family would be so kind, could they please go downstairs to the church hall and await them all for a meal the church women had prepared. Del knew exactly what this meant—there would be a vote taken by the congregation right then and there. Del smiled, made the announcement, gave the benediction, then proceeded down the aisle, glad-handing folks as he went, then gently grabbing Connie Jo by the arm and escorting her downstairs.

"We're in," he said. "This is just a formality. They wouldn't send us down here if everyone was going to come in afraid to look us in the eye and embarrass us. Plus, I know that sermon knocked the ball out of the park."

Connie thought she would leap out of her skin with excitement.

---

Returning home to Montgomery to begin packing, a knock came on the door. It was Vardemen and Exa Shirey. Vardemen spoke, softly and respectfully.

"We just wanted to come by and say our good-byes. We're both sorry things didn't turn out as they should have, but we wish the two of you well. We pray for you two as well as the boys. Del, if you let God use you the way He wants to, big things can happen for you and they *will* happen. I pray that God blesses you and your family. You have a wife who's very supportive of you, and a lot of ministers would love to have a wife like her that is one-hundred-percent with her husband in the ministry. You can't find that just anywhere."

Del Mobley never looked up from his work, just grunted an acknowledgement that someone had been in the room saying something, and nothing more. Exa turned to Connie Jo and embraced her, both women's eyes filling with tears.

"You be good, now. The Lord is watching over you in whatever you do—I know that."

"I know that, too, Exa. Bless you. I couldn't have gotten through this past year or so without you. I'll love you forever."

With that, Exa Shirey broke down as if at a funeral, filled with remorse, guilt, sadness and regret.

Throughout, Del remained silent and standoffish—downright rude, in fact. Once they'd left, Del turned his vehemence on Connie Jo. "The only reason he ever wanted you to work for him was because you're pretty. You're a lot prettier than that sow of a cousin of mine. You're naïve and sweet and he wanted you."

"Del," she said, "that's your own family you're talking about. That's crazy talk."

"Connie Jo, I've watched him look at you. I've watched them all look at you. They look you up and down every time you walk into that church. They've been doing that ever since I got here, which means they were doing it long before I arrived. All those other men want is to get what they want and you know what that is."

"Del, that's horrible. Those people are my friends. They

are fine, Christian people. I'm sure it would kill them to know you would even think such things of them. Vardemen is family and he tried to be your best friend here in Montgomery. Is this how it's gonna be once we get to Florida? Is it?"

Del Mobley snickered derisively. "In Florida, I'll be running the show. Not just my wife, but the entire church. You are going to be a full-time pastor's wife and your life will be different. God is calling me to this ministry and I will run it the way God wants me to."

## Chapter Nineteen

The Second Baptist Bible Church of Gainesville was a modest parish that did not have a pastorium, so Del Mobley, his wife, Connie Jo, and their two sons, B.J. and Gabe, initially moved into a cramped, little apartment. With the modest salary the position paid, most all of Brother Del's predecessors had lived likewise, but Del had big plans for Second Baptist and in turn, big plans for himself and his family.

"Connie Jo, I'm calling the bank. We need to cash in a couple more CDs. We need a home, not this little hovel. A man in my position has to exude power and strength. How are the people of this parish going to pick themselves up and build something when their pastor is living like someone who just got off the boat?"

There was no acknowledgement that the money was Connie Jo's; there never was. There was "I" and the occasional "we," which was another way of expressing "I" but in the form of the royal "we," for Del Mobley did not seek counsel with his wife, or with anyone else for that matter.

"Del, *another* CD?" Connie Jo whined. "You made us get rid of all our furniture before we left Alabama and we didn't get near what it was worth when we sold it. That was the furniture you made us buy less than a year ago. It was so new, it still *smelled* new! Now, on top of a new house, we're going to have to furnish it. We could have used that furniture. We can't afford all this, all at once."

"The apartment was furnished. You said that yourself."

"I said we should put that furniture into storage. This is probably nothing more than an excuse to go buy more and newer stuff. I'm beginning to think you're a shopaholic!"

"Storage is a bad bargain. Besides, now we have an excuse to buy all new things—decorate the new place right. We'll need at least two CDs, maybe three. This church is dirt poor and it'll stay that way so long as it thinks small. The same goes for us."

"But Del," she complained, "the money keeps going out, but it never comes back."

Del Mobley looked at her with condescension and disappointment. "You don't believe in me, do you? You don't think I can do this. You're hanging on to that money as if I'm some beggar at the door and not your husband, whom you vowed to honor and obey."

Like with all such arguments, Connie Jo felt as she did, never truly agreeing with Del even in losing the battle, but in the end, Del was big and Del was strong and Del did what he pleased. While married to Ben, Connie Jo had learned to turn her back on her husband when they fought, to toss in a spicy zinger or two, to refuse to talk to him for a time. When she did, Ben always had melted. Like any other couple, she had not always won those spats either, but win or lose, Ben always had known she was a person of value and he'd always wanted to be within her love and her heart.

Del Mobley showed far less insecurity in their relationship, ruling with an iron fist and treating Connie Jo like an easily replaced employee or a child. No matter what she tried, it never worked on Del as it had with Ben. Ben had wanted her to love him; Del wanted her to obey him. It became more and more apparent that Del did not love her in the way that Ben had, for love was surrender and Del Mobley surrendered to no one. Perhaps this was part of his allure, yet as time went by, Connie Jo kept wondering how much of herself was disappearing along the way.

Her savings was being eaten away bit by bit. No longer did she have the wherewithal and the security of knowing that she and boys would be safe and secure for life. New money would have to come in, but Del Mobley had yet to prove he was capable of bringing it in. Yet, he thought big—far bigger than Ben Filer ever had—and he was so darn majestic at times, especially when he was in the pulpit or on the altar, preaching. At those times, he could have said he would someday be president of the United States and the boast would have been believable, and so Connie Jo continued to follow him and forgive his prideful transgressions. Men of that stature rarely apologized.

And so they soon moved in to a brand-new home in a brand-new development, and the place was impressive—everything new and shiny. On one level, it pleased Connie Jo greatly—that was, of course, until she realized it was just a figment, a thing that wasn't truly theirs because it had eaten up so much of their security yet still did not belong solely to them, but mostly to the bank. How on Earth would they be able to keep up the payments? But Brother Del had faith, and thus, Connie Jo was presumed to have none, and for this she was made to feel somehow less spiritual, less wise in the eyes of the Lord and in the eyes of His messenger, Brother Del Mobley.

The boys, B.J. and Gabe, settled into their new school happily, but time at home started to settle into new patterns as well. Del ignored them by and large, except to thrash them when they acted like children around him. When he was out, they laughed and played, but once he returned, the house was full of dead silence. At dinner, all sorts of new rules were created. One night, B.J.'s hand was slapped as he reached for the water pitcher. "You eat your food first, then you can have a drink."

"But my mouth is dry. I need a drink."

Del quickly whacked him on the side of his face with the back of his hand. "Don't you sass me, boy. You sit upright at the table and you obey orders, and one of those orders is you eat first, then drink. You don't mix food and drink at the same time."

"Del, that makes no sense to me…" Connie Jo would have said more, but she was met by a stare that could have turned boiling water to ice.

"Do you want the back of my hand, too? This is my table, my house and my rules. These boys are gonna grow up soft and disrespectful unless I lay down the law. The big one's already a pansy momma's boy."

Connie Jo wanted to say more, but she knew she could not take Del Mobley in a physical fight, and the vision of her being beaten again in front of her boys—for it had happened many times over the course of their first year of marriage—dissuaded her from continuing.

Del plainly favored Gabriel, her youngest, for what reason she could only surmise. Perhaps it was that B.J. still bore the first name of his real father, Ben, and thus reminded Del always that he was not his own, but yet another possession he had somehow inherited. Along with that, B.J. remembered his daddy far more than little Gabe, and would have been more likely to hang on to those memories. Thus, he stood as a threat to this new world order.

Gabe, on the other hand, could possibly have been molded into Del's own image, the thought of which revolted Connie Jo at times. When Del acted like such a dictator, she at least felt that it was her and her two boys against the world, but if Del managed to peel off Gabe and turn him against her, too, what then would she have? The thought drove her to deep, depressive thoughts.

Fairly soon, Del's dictatorial ways spread to the church itself. It was as if everything became a clone of his marriage. He created rules that made sense only to him. He spent money that wasn't there, and when he did, he reminded the church that it was, in his eyes, his money and not theirs and how dare they question his authority? "God is over me and I am over you, and that is the line of succession," he'd bellow. "God will lead me and I will lead you. You are in sore need of strong leadership and that's just what you're going to get. I am on fire for the Lord and with God's help, you will see miracles in this church."

"Amen, Brother Mobley!" And just as soon as the uprising had begun, he had extinguished it with his rhetoric. Del Mobley smiled inside. This was the way to everything he'd ever wanted.

Indeed, the little church grew. One topic Del Mobley vacilated on was the depth of personal involvement of his pretty, young wife, Connie Jo. At first, he had warned the church elders that his wife was not to have any role of leadership within the church, had tried to persuade them that were anything to happen to him, or were he to succeed so greatly that he was called to move on and move up to a larger congregation, Second Baptist would be without just one but two church leaders.

Nonetheless, women within the church began to notice the goodness, skill and charisma of Sister Connie Jo and began leaning on her to help with church school, youth groups, choir and other such activities. Each time, Del blustered, but on this he was more prone to give in, as Connie Jo's talents made *him* look good. Still, he always greeted her when she returned from these forays to the outside world with snide quips such as, "Who's your boyfriend *now?*" or, "Are you through tantalizing all the men of Gainesville?"

"Del, half the time you say such hurtful things, I'm out with only women and children. Why does your mind work in such ways?"

Del often answered, "A, I'm a man, and B, I was married before, remember?"

"Did Vivian step out on you? Is that it?"

At the mere mention of Vivian's name, Del's eyes would turn to slits. It was one thing when he brought it up, but her name was never to touch Connie Jo's sweet lips. "I don't want to talk about it," he would grumble, and then he would spend the rest of the day and night ignoring her quite purposefully.

Between the two of them, everything was church, church, church, and their success at Second Baptist became quite obvious. At times, Connie Jo cynically wondered if it were all due to the newness of it all—the new preacher with his new wife and family. Old church members came out more out of curiosity than anything else, she surmised, to see what these new folks looked like and to form an impression.

But many of them stayed, for Brother Mobley's

preaching was moving and spirited each and every week. Even Connie Jo was enthralled, wondering how he could muster up the spirit so dynamically week in and week out. She rarely saw him practicing or spending huge amounts of time studying, writing or preparing his sermons. It was as if he were channeling God and God spoke through him in a way that grabbed on to the ears of every man, woman and child in that chapel and forced them to listen up!

Churches can be a place of petty gossip, too, but somehow everyone took a genuine liking to Sister Connie Jo, and she brought the women of the parish together, getting them active and spreading her genuine spirit of love and neighborliness. In many ways, these were the golden days of their marriage, as Connie Jo saw it. She'd begun to accept Del's quirks—the jealousy, the quickness to anger, the authoritarian stance, especially with the boys. The boys accepted his treatment as young children are wont to do. Deep down, they thought they were loved and so they forgave the occasional butt lashings and accepted that although they may not have totally agreed at the time, it must have been their fault and they somehow deserved it.

This was the part that Connie Jo had the hardest time with. She could never picture Ben hitting them or being as conservative with them as Del. Del seemed to want them out of sight and out of mind as much as possible. When he was around, he wanted not a sound from them. All of their behaviors were being molded so that they would be like little adults in children's bodies, not children at all. He gave them both television sets for their bedrooms so that they would retreat to those rooms immediately after dinner and thus be out of his sight for the rest of the night. He was one of the few parents Connie Jo knew who actually encouraged his kids to watch lots of TV, and it broke her heart. There was little to no family time, and growing up, family had been so important to her.

# Chapter Twenty

Just as the congregation grew, after a year or so, Brother Mobley—for he no longer wished to be called "Brother Del," a moniker he now felt was too familiar and thus beneath him—started down the path of some of his old, bad habits. First, he asked—actually demanded—that he have at least one day completely off from work, where he would not even be reachable by phone. The board of deacons was none too happy, but Del Mobley pounded his fist and said, "Look around you. All that you see is what I created. Even the Lord Himself rested for one day," and reluctantly, they let it be so.

Soon, the sleeping late began. Del's day rarely began before noon, far different than those first heady months where he truly was on fire for the Lord and he seemed to spend every ounce of his energy on the Lord's work. This, too, did not go unnoticed by the church elders, yet again, Del bulled them down with his bluster, much as he did within his own home.

One night, Connie Jo sat in bed reading, wondering to herself why Del was, again, not joining her, as the hour was late and he used to come to bed around that time. The boys had been asleep since 8:00 p.m., since that was Del's strict orders. This could have and should have meant that she and her husband would spend some couple time together, yet this rarely occurred anymore, as she was often asleep by the time he came to bed. Even before this, Del would stay downstairs most every evening, ordering her upstairs so as not to disturb him as he prepared his sermons, and then he would come up to her in a very amorous mood. The passion he showed for her made her feel good and made her feel wanted in a way that wives should feel, and so it pleased her, although she wished she could spend some time just hanging out together, talking and being close during the earlier parts of the evening.

This night, she decided to tiptoe downstairs to see what he was up to and, perhaps, persuade him to come upstairs or else engage her in his endeavors. The closer she got, the more she was able to hear sounds from the television set. The volume was turned down low—she assumed this to be a courtesy that she, in fact, appreciated, given that she might be trying to sleep and the boys most certainly were already asleep. But with every step, the sounds became clearer. There was no music track, no laugh track, and no commercials. Instead, there was incessant moaning and groaning, interrupted by occasional profanity.

"What are you watching?" she asked as she was finally at the base of the stairs. It was a rhetorical question, for from her vantage point she could see quite clearly what he was doing: watching pornography. Her mouth was agape and dry, fearful and repulsed, as Del made no quick moves to disguise what he was doing. Instead, he ignored her, displaying an attitude of being impervious to her judgment of him.

Connie Jo stepped even closer. "Del, why are you watching that smut?"

Again, he ignored her, and she wondered if it was something that had come on the cable TV after he had dozed off in front of it. But no, the closer she came, the more obvious it was that Reverend Delbert Mobley was wide awake, glued to the action on the tube, belligerently refusing to acknowledge her presence or answer her queries.

"Del, I'm talking to you!"

Finally, without removing his eyes from the explicit writhing going on on the screen, he replied, "I don't have to answer to you. If you want to stay, stay. If not, leave me alone."

Connie Jo was without words. Each Sunday, this mountain of a man preached vehemently against the sins of the flesh, against pornography, smoking, drinking, all sorts of moral indiscretions, yet here he was, slouched down in his chair, watching the most vulgar actions imaginable. A glass of wine sat on the end table next to him.

"You're…you're a hypocrite! What is your problem? You should be working or you should be in bed. This is wrong, all wrong."

"Judge not lest ye be judged. Maybe this is your fault."

"I, I…" but Connie Jo had no more words. How effortlessly he staved her off. How comfortable he felt within his own actions. If she thought it was hypocrisy, that was her problem, for obviously he disagreed and his was the only opinion that mattered—his and God's, and since Del felt strongly that God spoke through him personally, whatever God found amiss with Del was just between the two of them.

Disgusted, Connie Jo turned and went back upstairs and attempted to fall asleep but failed miserably. A few hours later, Del slid under the covers. It was past three-thirty in the morning. He'd had enough wine that the smell lingered on his breath. His presence revolted her.

The next morning, Connie Jo got up at her usual early time to have the boys off to school. Months earlier, Del would have been downstairs shortly after they had left, around eight o'clock, but this was no longer the routine. Connie Jo went about her ministrations—reading the news, cleaning, even going to the grocery store. She made herself lunch. Eventually, around one-thirty, Del Mobley finally appeared, washed and dressed and ready for work.

"Half day today?" she asked sarcastically. She still feared

him, but she felt little to no respect for him that day. He ignored her. "I have a handful of messages from congregants. People have been looking for their minister," she said as she waved a fistful of pink slips of paper.

He looked at her as if he were hung over, which he may indeed have been—mean, yet quiet. "I want the phone taken off the hook until I wake up. And I'll wake up whenever I damn well please. This is my house and it is my church. If somebody's dying, they can call the police or the ambulance. Outside of that, it obviously can wait, 'cause it surely isn't life or death."

Connie Jo was still too sickened by what she'd seen the night before to want to harangue him. She ignored him, much as he often did her.

Later that evening, once the boys were in bed, she again came downstairs and again found the same thing she'd seen the night before: Del watching porn and drinking wine.

"Is this the new thing? Is this what life is going to be like around here? Staying up all night watching smut, then sleeping away the entire morning? That's no way for a minister to act and it's going to get you fired."

"You want me to turn it off?"

"Yes, I want you to turn it off."

"Get upstairs. I'll be right there."

Connie Jo turned and went back from whence she came. About thirty minutes later, Del walked into their bedroom and was soon under the covers, holding her tightly. "Now I'm ready for you."

"Del, get away from me. You're disgusting. You need some counseling."

"And my side of the story will be that my wife won't love me. Once I say that, what do you think some counselor is going to say? Better I stay downstairs than I go out wildcatting with some floozy," he said, and he grabbed her even more tightly.

Like on the night he had raped her when her ribs were broken and she was concussed, he had his way with her against her will. She stared up at the ceiling and prayed for it to be over as quickly as possible. *My God, why hast Thou forsaken me?*

The next morning, Connie Jo peeled Del off of her and prepared the boys for school. This time, she decided she would not simply ignore Del and let him waste the day away. Each time she confronted him, she knew she was poking a bear with a stick, but she was reaching the point of no longer caring about herself and her own well-being. He'd beaten her, he'd raped her, he'd taken everything from her and enslaved her. All she had left were the boys and her life.

The boys. Oh, God, that stopped her in her tracks. The boys. If anything ever happened to her, the boys would be at his mercy. She was all that stood between Del and her precious sons and no, she could not take herself out of that equation. They even had his name now, much to her chagrin.

When she'd called Ben's people to discuss it with them, they'd been adamantly against it. They had always loved her so, but when it became apparent that she was not empowered to prevent it from happening, they cut her off, saying as much as, "So long as you're alive, this is your decision as much as your new husband's. If you go along with it, it's the same as if you simply made it happen yourself. Those boys were Ben's only legacy. Now, you're stealing his birthright. We can't abide by that. You do that, we've got nothing to talk about from here on in."

Connie Jo had been heartbroken. As for Del, he was just callously pleased that he had won again.

Connie Jo climbed the stairs and entered her bedroom, where Del lay sleeping and snoring. "Get up," she said as she shook him. "Get up and go to work."

Del Mobley rolled over slightly to face her and grumbled, "You want me, you come in here and keep me company, otherwise, go the hell away," and he rolled back away from her again.

Connie Jo stared down at him as if he were a puzzle to be figured out. Oh, how she loathed him in so many ways. Yet what were her options? If she left him, what would that say about her? Is that what a Christian woman would do? To most of the world, he was this human dynamo for Christ, a man of the cloth. He sure didn't look like it from this angle, but Connie Jo had to live in the real world, and what she saw behind closed doors was not what the real world saw. Maybe every preacher's wife dealt with the human behind the preacher's mask.

When he rose up on Sunday mornings, Del Mobley was filled with the spirit and he imparted that spirit to the congregants of the community. Wasn't that a good thing? Wasn't that the righteous, godly thing for a man to do?

Conflicted, she gently pulled the covers aside and joined him in bed. It felt silly and strange; the sun was well up in the sky. She'd taken the phone off the hook as he'd requested, so they wouldn't be disturbed. Would he try to ravage her again as he had the night before?

At least he wasn't drunk now. But still, the image of him sitting there in front of that television, using such disgusting images in order to want to be with her, or having it fulfill him in place of her—it all nauseated her. But no, he did not start up with her. He rolled over and draped one big, burly paw over and around her, and she rolled over and away from him, annoyed by his morning breath.

*Maybe he'd be satisfied just cuddling,* she thought. Indeed, that seemed to be the case. But for as much as she felt this was acceptable for a time, the day was still churning forward and there was much to do—much that *he* should have been doing. Whenever she put the phone back in the cradle, it began ringing like mad and she had to make up all sorts of excuses as to why Brother Mobley couldn't be reached at such reasonable times as ten-thirty in the morning.

He began snoring. Connie Jo just lay there, unable to extricate herself from his heavy grip. Hours went by. She could not sleep; she'd slept more than enough the night before. She stared at the wall, a woman trapped, wasting her life away. It became like a metaphor for all that was going on around her. Del was losing his grip on this good thing they had. The days off, the mornings off, the rules, the dictatorial ways. Soon the parish would tire of his nonsense and he'd be out of a job again. It was like a car wreck she could see coming from a mile away, yet could do nothing about. Del Mobley: Reverend Trainwreck.

# Chapter Twenty-One

Del returned home from a meeting with the board of deacons. "I just told those knuckleheads I can't be working night and day, day and night, and never making time for my family."

Connie Jo tried to stifle a laugh. She knew how hard her brother, Rusty, worked at his parish in St. Augustine; he worked rings around Del. Still, there was no reason to laugh, for crying would have been more appropriate. *He's going to blow it,* she kept saying to herself. *He's going to blow it and then what will we have?*

"The other day I went out for a ride. I found a nice lake about fifty miles from here. They have some cabins for sale. Nice for fishing and weekending. They have them wired for telephones, but once I buy one, I'll just rip the darn wire out."

"What are you talking about?" Connie Jo asked, perplexed.

"Haven't you been following me? I told the deacons I needed some family time. I got a young wife and two young boys. I can't be an absentee father…"

Connie Jo again tried to stifle laughter. "Father." He was no more a father to B.J. and Gabe than he was a rodeo clown.

Del rambled on. "We'll take a day or two off during the week, and then go on Saturdays and holidays as well. I'll teach the boys to fish."

"Let me get this straight: You're going to buy us a fishing cabin fifty miles from here. A second home."

"Well, I don't know if I'd call it a home. It isn't as nice as this place, but yes, call it what you will. A cabin. I'm buying us a cabin."

"With what? We can barely pay the mortgage on *this* place."

"I called the bank," Del said. "Cashed in two more CDs."

"Del, that's *my* money! You should discuss these things with me!"

Del Mobley's face hardened. "It's *our* money. It's *my* money. Don't let me tell you again how a Christian family works. I don't need your permission to do what I feel is best."

"Del, it's not permission—it's just communication. You never discuss anything with me. You just go off and do whatever you please and I don't get considered at all."

The argument went on for a time, but it was pointless. Del had again absconded with her money and there was little Connie Jo felt she could do. With each passing day; with each action on his part, Connie Jo kept seeing the warning light flashing: Danger! Danger!

With a long face, Connie Jo rode on out with Del to see this "family present" he was so excited about. Gabe and B.J., of course, knew nothing of the tension going on between their two parents, but instead focused on all the jabbering Del was doing about fun, sun and fishing.

Once they arrived, Del did make it a fun day for them, teaching them how to cast, how to bait a hook and how to reel 'em in. Connie Jo sat on a large rock nearby, still stewing in her own juices. *My money probably bought the poles and the gear, too,* she thought.

She looked at her reflection in the water and didn't like what stared back at her. It was a bitter, unhappy woman, the kind of person she'd felt she would never be. Oh, how she noticed all those fishwives with their constant frowns, old before their time, making the world miserable around them. Was she turning into one of those women? Was this how those women came to be? Was she, perhaps, too concerned with the vagaries of the future and allowing those insecurities to make her lose out on life?

Del preached faith all the time and he bellowed it in their home every time Connie Jo doubted him or was cynical about his ways. Was he on to something? She looked at her laughing boys, her smiling husband, and then back into the water at herself. Visual inventory: happy people, happy person, sad person. She was the odd one out.

Over the next few months, Del spent enormous amounts of time at the cabin, time that he should have spent working and building his parish. The initial boost he had given the congregation had begun to wane. No longer were new faces filling the pews. His sermons were still preached with vigor, but a congregation asks for more than that from its spiritual leader. It asks for time spent consoling the sick, the bereaved and the troubled, and Del Mobley was rarely around for that, and so they strayed.

Del began to invite influential church members to join him and his family at the cabin and indeed, it posed, for a while, another new treat for some. But like all new things, it got old fast and what was left was the bad taste in many people's mouths that their leader, Brother Mobley, was not there for them and did not love them as they needed to be loved, and so they became embittered.

When he did make courtesy calls to the congregants, he began to drag Connie Jo along. She enjoyed it and, in fact, she managed to stave off numerous complaints about Del by being there to smooth over his sometimes-rough edges, his temper and his need to feel empowered. But this, too, digressed into something negative. It didn't matter if she was in the middle of preparing a meal or cleaning the house; if Del decided he needed to go to the church or visit a parishioner, Connie Jo had to drop what she was doing immediately or else Del would refuse to go, blaming his failure to perform his duties on her.

"I thought you said you wanted to be a preacher's wife? Why won't you stand by me and do God's work?"

"I love doing God's work with you, Del, but must I be like a fireman, jumping up from every single thing I'm doing so that I can accompany you?"

Del harrumphed. "That's what they expect *me* to do. That's what *you* expect me to do. Why should you get off easy?"

"Del, it's your job, not mine. I'd be happy to help out from time to time, but I never knew of a minister's wife who had to be attached to his hip like you want me to be. You never acted this way before. What's with all this?"

Del's eyes narrowed to a squint. "I can just imagine what goes on around here when I'm out. Half the men in town must be calling and knocking on the door."

Connie Jo didn't know whether to laugh or cry. "Del, you know I'm not a runaround. I would never be unfaithful to you."

"It's not just up to you. It's all those other men. I don't feel comfortable leaving you out of my sight."

Connie Jo just stared at him incredulously. So this was the new rule—Del would only work if Connie Jo worked alongside him, like some sidekick whom he was never without. The stress was becoming overwhelming. If she did not do this, Del would be just the kind of person to adamantly refuse to do his duties, damning his job and their futures to hell. He'd somehow managed to put it all on her. The pressure, the pressure. It was a giant game of chicken, and her personal sense of responsibility would be her own downfall.

Del could allow it all to crumble around them, but Connie Jo had to think of the boys as well as herself. A fine mess. A fine mess indeed.

One of the most banal aspects of domestic life is the trip to the mailbox. Most days it contains nothing more than shopping circulars and other such junk mail, but as days went by, the mail to the Mobley home became lighter and lighter. No bills, it seemed, nor any checks, such as the ones Connie Jo was used to getting from Social Security as well as the insurance companies that handled her claims from Ben's death. "Del, how come we don't hardly get any mail anymore? All the bills and checks I usually get are never here."

Del Mobley nonchalantly answered, "I got us a post office box. Since I take of our books now, I just stop off every day or so and get the mail, then I sort it out and work everything out at my office at the church."

"Why'd you do that? Besides, I never see you doing our bookkeeping when you bring me to the church."

Del became huffy and impatient. "These are a bunch of stupid questions, you know that, Connie Jo? I don't drag you into the bathroom to watch me do my business, either. Doesn't mean I don't do it. Why are you always so suspicious?"

Connie Jo composed herself and tried to find the right

words. "Del, I've been married before and I'm used to a marriage being an open thing where we both know what's going on, especially when it comes to money. Why didn't you tell me you got a post office box? What if you were to drop dead tomorrow? I'd never even have known about it and I wouldn't be able to fetch our bills and checks."

"You planning on killing me?"

"Del! That's horrible. You know I'd never even think such a thing."

Del puffed out his chest menacingly and Connie Jo began to cower, recalling each and every one of the beatings he'd frequently given her. Even when his rage did not turn physical he had a way of getting inside her head, abusing her, making her feel so incredibly small and, worst of all, making her feel like a bad wife and a bad Christian. "You brought it up. Talking about me dropping dead. I ain't never talked about anything ever happening to you."

Connie Jo thought for a moment. "Oh yes you did. You brought it up when you put your name on every single thing of mine and the boys'. You brought it up when you made them take your name. You brought it up many a time."

He now stood over her, dead-faced. "I ain't got nobody but you. You got Robertses and Filers running around all over the place. But me, I only got you. Anything happens to me, don't take a genius to know all that's mine goes to you."

"But what about Vivian? And what about that girl, Rae?"

Del smiled deviously. "I got my paper, remember?" And he patted his breast pocket. His paper. His paper. He clung to that one piece of paper as if it somehow justified everything he ever did from there on in. Vivian's paper saying that they were divorced, that she had taken his child from him and that he was a virtuous man and she an unvirtuous woman.

Connie Jo wondered about Vivian and Rae just then, something she rarely did. She'd been married to Del for a few years now. She knew his nature, or at least she thought she did. There were times she wondered why she stayed in this marriage, how she loathed him so when he acted so brutish towards her and the boys. Had Vivian and Rae gone through the same thing? Was it that Vivian was simply a stronger woman than she, a woman who, when faced with the meanness that Del demonstrated on so many occasions, took their child and ran off to safety? For so long, Connie Jo had thought nothing but ill of the woman, but now she wondered: Did Vivian have it right all along?

# Chapter Twenty-Two

Day in and day out, Connie Jo's life revolved around being at Del's beck and call. She tried to accept it, to make the best of it, and the best of it was, indeed, rather good. She loved being a preacher's wife, and when she was doing the church's work she could immerse herself in it and feel like she was making a difference in people's lives.

Still, she worried about what each new day might bring. Del continued to work less and less. She often felt like a prisoner in her own home. If she was not glued to Del's side, she had to have the phone taken off the hook and thus was rarely ever able to make outgoing calls unless Del was standing right there, listening in on everything. She called her family from time to time, but with these calls being monitored, she could never open up and be herself—her old, jovial self. She also could not be truthful.

"How are things? You never sound like yourself these days, Connie Jo. Are you sure you're all right?"

"Yes, yes, everything's fine," she would lie, smiling nervously as Del stared, making sure she did not reveal too much.

Even when she saw them, Del was always around, making himself available to them but not to his responsibilities at the church. Her brother, Rusty, would make remarks, pointed remarks on occasion, that led Connie Jo to believe that word around the area was that Del had gone from growing Second Baptist to destroying it bit by bit.

"Del, my sister can serve snacks just fine. Why don't you go on back to work? We're fine here."

"Why don't you go back to *your* church? Who's minding the store there?" he replied.

"I got no complaints from my people. Course, I hear some things are rocky out here in Gainesville," Rusty responded, making a point while trying not to become too confrontational during a family get-together.

Del quickly rose and looked ready to explode, but Connie Jo put her hand on Rusty's and whispered loudly to him, "Now don't you come in here making trouble. Things are fine."

With that, Del sat back down, pleased that his wife had sided with him and not her own brother. "Yeah, you listen to your sister. Things are fine. If we need your help, we know where to find you."

One day, Connie Jo made the mistake of not taking the phone off the hook before Del arose. She was in the kitchen and he was still in bed when it rang. She jumped, quickly answering it so that Del would not be angered.

"Hello? May I speak to Delbert Mobley?"

"This is his wife. May I help you?" Connie Jo said in a quiet voice, praying that Del would not rouse.

"This is Chase Visa. There is a card registered in your husband's name that is presently ninety days in arrears. The minimum payment is one thousand, five hundred forty-eight dollars. When can we expect that payment?"

*God,* Connie Jo thought. *Over fifteen hundred dollars. And that's just the minimum. He must have tens of thousands of dollars in credit-card debt. And what about everything else? We have two mortgages…and car payments…and…*

"Hello? Mrs. Mobley?" The voice brought her back to earth.

"Ma'am, I'm sorry, but my husband is not here at the moment. May I take your number and have him call you back?"

The woman on the other end of the line gave Connie Jo an 800 number but was sure to add, "We've tried to reach him numerous times. As his spouse, you are also liable for this debt. When can we expect his call?"

Connie Jo held the receiver as if it were a dead pigeon,

something she simply wanted to get out of her hand as quickly as possible. "Soon," she whispered, then hung up the phone.

Any other wife would have immediately rushed upstairs and woken her husband, telling him in no uncertain terms that he had troubles and he'd better take care of them. But other women weren't married to Del Mobley. He'd crush her, she was sure of that. The point of the matter would be lost in his erratic accusations of "how dare you pick up the phone when I expressly told you not to" and so on.

Instead, she cowered on the living-room chair at the bottom of the staircase, listening intently to hear if Del would come down. She had never been so scared in her life—scared of Del's rage for her answering the phone, scared of confronting Del in order to better understand where their finances were at, and scared of how badly he was managing those finances. It was almost as if she didn't want to know; it all sounded so bad.

And so she sat. She sat and she prayed. She prayed for it all to be some sort of misunderstanding. She prayed to be put out of her pain and her misery. She prayed that God would watch over her and keep her from harm. But moreover, she simply prayed.

Connie Jo went that entire day and night waiting for Del to say something about the phone call, but it was not to be. She knew she should confront him and give him the message, but that would only open up the entire beehive. Instead, she did nothing more than cherish every moment that did not involve Del thrashing her or haranguing her.

She thought of somehow slipping away, bundling up the kids and running away from him forever. But Del would know exactly where to find her, for she loved her family and no longer had any independent resources. He would find her with her parents or one of her siblings and then what? All she could envision was a bloodbath, for Del seemed capable of impassioned rage that might know no end. It was his passion that had attracted her to him in the beginning, but now she saw the other side of passion—how it could fill a person with crazy, irrational thoughts. Del Mobley wanted what he wanted, and he wanted it his way. If he did not get it, there was always hell to pay.

The next day, Connie Jo made certain to have the phone off the hook. She did not want another call, even if taking the call might save her from personal financial ruin. She prayed that Del would somehow be a real man and take care of it.

Instead, Del awoke and announced another fishing trip to the cabin with her and the boys.

"Del, don't you think maybe we've been spending enough time out there? I mean, if instead of fishing, you were out in the field for the church, maybe things would pick up."

He eyed her suspiciously. "Things are fine. Church is

doing alright. What's the use of working your life away? They ain't gonna pay me more unless a hundred more people join up and that ain't gonna happen. I've beaten the bushes for those people. It is what it is. I gotta smell the roses while I can."

Smell the roses. All he seemed to do was smell roses. Del came alive on Sunday mornings, when he could get up on his stage—the altar—and perform. But ministering to people went far beyond the performance. It involved caring for people one on one, but this did not appear to appeal to Del Mobley. Del was like Elvis—alive on the stage, but Elvis did not do interviews.

The times at the cabin were still fun for the boys—the only times they seemed to be able to relax around Del. This was good and not good. Connie Jo could point to so few moments in her day-to-day life where she felt truly happy and at ease, and now she could see that B.J. and Gabe were growing up in much the same way—happy fishing at the cabin or away from Del, but tentative and afraid of whuppings just about any other time they were around him.

*Sad, so sad,* she thought. What kind of men would they grow up to be? Would they disrespect their women, dominate them as Del did to her? Or would their cowering continue into all aspects of their lives, making them spineless, fearful people who would be anemic and ineffective in all that they would do? How could a man of God so poison everything around him?

Still, for the boys' sakes, Connie Jo put on a brave and

smiling face as they all cast their lines and soaked in the sunshine. At the end of the day, they squeezed into the car, when suddenly Del said, "I think I forgot something back in the cabin. Y'all stay here. I'll be right back."

No one ventured to argue, and he was back about five minutes later, a bit nervous and twitchy, but back nonetheless. Another wife would have at least made polite conversation about why he went back, but Connie Jo now censored everything that came out of her mouth and no, asking such a thing would fall into Del's category of "things that of are none of your damn business," and so she let it go.

She let far too much go and she wondered, as time went by, why exactly she did that. But then, she thought of the good works she was doing as a preacher's wife and how the boys had a father—not a good father, but wasn't a bad father better than none at all? How much harder would it be to meet another man once she'd been married twice before, and with two boys—older boys by now—attached to her as part of the bargain?

Still, as they rode home, Connie Jo looked from time to time at Del Mobley as they rode in silence. When he wanted to, he could still be that man who could get down on his knees before her and tell her how much he loved her. Those moments were farther and farther between now, but maybe that was how marriage worked. Her time with Ben had been so short, maybe things would have evolved with him in much the same way.

If Del had grown tired of her, maybe that was partially

her fault. Perhaps it was all a matter of how he expressed himself. He was so darn jealous; maybe that was all about how infatuated he still was with her. The more she stared, the more she mused about what a complicated man Del Mobley was, and how his complexities and her desire to understand were a lot of the reasons why she stayed with him.

That and the preaching. Oh, how she still sat in enthralled rapture when he preached. So long as he could still get up and do that each Sunday, she might have put up with just about anything. No matter how badly he misbehaved or mistreated her during the week, when he got up and preached the gospel on Sundays, she forgot all the bad things and got taken up in the moment. She saw no hypocrisy because when he opened his mouth on these mornings, it no longer seemed to be his own voice but God's voice speaking, and how could she ever question her love for God?

When they returned home, Connie Jo, as was her routine, put the phone back on the hook and waited for the inevitable slew of calls and Del's predictably bad mood at having to take them. He wouldn't even acquiesce to an answering machine. So, it came as no surprise when, less than five minutes after the phone went back on, it rang. She answered it.

"Sister Connie, this is Ada down at the church. We've been getting calls here for Brother Mobley. There's a fire!"

"A fire? Where?" Connie Jo asked.

"Your cabin out of town. Are you all right? I was so afraid something had happened to y'all. You were there today, weren't you?"

Connie Jo's hand shook with a case of nerves. "Yes, we were just there."

"Well, bless the Lord, you're all right. It's a terrible thing, a terrible thing. Here, I'll give you the number of their emergency services department. They can tell you what's going on."

The next day, Del Mobley ran around talking to police, fire and insurance people, but for once, he allowed Connie Jo to stay at home alone without being on a virtual leash beside him. She did something brassy yet, to her, logical by leaving the phone on in case something relating to the fire came through. She took calls all day long from parishioners, but nothing directly relating to the fire. Yet something else went through her head as the day went by and she stared and stared at the phone as if it were a live creature: Not a single call from a bill collector came, either. Not a single one.

# Chapter Twenty-Three

Despite no longer having his beloved fishing cabin, there was a renewed spring in Del Mobley's step in the weeks after the fire. Still, he did not replace his time at the cabin with greater time spent at this job. He seemed to spend even more time staying up late at night, watching pornography and sleeping until the afternoon. The board of deacons' enthusiasm for his leadership at Second Baptist continued to wane, and Connie Jo worried that the day would soon be nigh when they would be asking for his resignation.

"You need a job."

"What?" Connie Jo said, dumbstruck by what Del had just uttered.

"I don't mean a job in the purest sense. I mean a business. You're so talented and special, Connie Jo, I feel I've been holding you back."

Connie Jo looked at him strangely. It was indeed a compliment, but one that came from way out in left field. He was always so jealous, keeping her cocooned at home like some sort of prisoner or else permanently attached to him.

"What would you like to do? If money were no object, what would be your dream?" His eyes flashed and his teeth shined.

Connie Jo, still taken aback, thought for a moment. "I don't know, Del. I always wanted to be a baker, maybe have myself a cake shop or something like that. Maybe a beautician. I used to cut hair. I cut my sisters' hair sometimes when we were younger. I still cut the boys' hair. It saves us a little money and I'm pretty good at it."

"Okay, then, pick one and let's do it. Spread your wings and fly, little dove." He chuckled lovingly.

Connie Jo investigated her options. Still, she was perplexed. This suggestion was so unlike Del. She liked it, she really did, but it followed no pattern she was used to in their marriage. Since the fire, though, Del had a newfound inner calm that she liked. Strangely, she'd assumed he'd be frustrated that he no longer had his getaway place.

Connie Jo researched, made calls and told Del she was leaning towards hair styling. It would require a license and some schooling—around a year or two's worth. He smiled and continued to encourage her.

"What about owning your own shop? What's involved in that?" he asked.

"They say you can own a shop without a license so long as you have licensed staff. It'd be just like buying any other kind of business. People invest in businesses all the time, I guess."

"Fine, fine," he answered, and Connie Jo felt it best to accept this prize treatment without asking too many questions. *Find your own way to happiness,* she thought. If this was an avenue Del was opening up to her, what harm could there be in her taking it?

A few days later, Del took her out for a drive. He stopped on Second Avenue, parked the car, and said to Connie Jo, smiling, "Step on out." She noticed nothing particularly unique about where they were; they drove around there often. "Anything come to mind?" he asked.

"Like what?"

"Keep looking," he answered, still smiling, still acting like he was about to get down on one knee and ask her to marry him all over again.

Finally, Connie Jo said, "Alright, I give up. What am I supposed to be seeing?"

With an impresario's flourish, Del waved his arm and said, "This is now yours. Name it what you will." Behind him was a beauty shop called "Delphine's," a nice-looking place that appeared to be open for business.

"I don't understand."

"Delphine is retiring. I got a lead from someone at the

church. I bought it for you. The staff is licensed and they'll probably be happy to stay on, if you want them. It's up to you." His grin went from ear to ear as he was in his element, standing bigger than life in front of this new trinket he presented to her.

Connie Jo was dumbstruck. "You bought me a hair salon?"

"Yup."

"How?" It was the simplest one-word question she could come up with, with the possible exception of "why?"

"A business is an investment. You sorta said so yourself. This is an investment. Stocks can go up and down, but with a business, your fortune is in your own hands. I'm betting on you, darlin'. Everybody loves you. I'm sure if you took over this place, you'd make a go of it. Doesn't it make you happy?"

Del's enthusiasm was contagious, particularly since he seemed to place all his pride upon her, how much he thought of her and how much he loved her. How could she possibly say "no"?

"How…How did we manage to pay for this?" she stammered, thinking for a moment about the credit-card call she'd received a while back.

"We still have some money in the bank, and I got the insurance money from the cabin."

Much as she hated to, Connie Jo mused cynically. *Money in the bank…mine. Insurance money…Why doesn't he just go out and buy another cabin? That's much more like him.*

But the taste of sugar is sweet, and this was, outside of her cynicism, such a wonderful thing. She'd no longer be a caged bird. She'd be keeping busy, meeting people, earning her own money. Whatever self-esteem she'd lost in the time she'd been with Del Mobley might possibly have come rushing back. That would have been nice.

And if anything ever had happened, anything bad where she felt she was at the end of her rope with Del, she'd have something of her own to fall back upon. She was sure Del wasn't thinking in those terms, but that was *his* problem as Connie Jo saw it. From then on, either he'd treat her right or else she'd have options of her own. That sounded good in her mind.

Over the next few weeks, Connie Jo threw herself into becoming a hairstylist and an entrepreneur. She enrolled in beauty school—$7,200—and set about establishing the shop. She met the other stylists and liked them all, at least enough to want to give them a try.

Continuity in a business like this was important. What she didn't need was for one of the other girls to quit and take all her clients with her. Outside of that, the shop was pretty much a turnkey operation, not in need of much except to change the name. And so, in almost no time at all, she was now the proprietor of "Connie Jo's". It felt good; it felt real good.

Throughout the transition, Del was there every single step of the way, which made her feel good, real good, although at night, once exhaustion had overtaken her and she lay in bed waiting for sweet sleep, she wondered, *I go to that shop and stay there from eight in the morning to seven at night, six days a week, and Del is right there the whole time, helping me out. How can he do that? Did he ask for a vacation? Is the church alright with this?*

Another woman would have rolled over and verbalized these queries, but Del was already snoring, unused to working such long hours, and besides, it would only anger him. Furthermore, it would be like looking a gift horse in the mouth. He really was a help, as she knew nothing about setting up a business and everything was happening so fast. If she'd done this on her own she would have spent about a year planning it, but instead, she was handed a *fait accompli:* Surprise! I bought you a business. Begin.

As soon as the place actually opened for business with Connie Jo in charge, things finally began to reveal themselves. Del was still there, looking odd—a man hanging around a women's hair salon all day long. He didn't bother Connie Jo much but drove the receptionist to distraction, hovering over her shoulder as she took calls, made appointments and, most of all, took in the money.

"I'll be keeping the books," he said to Connie Jo after only one day.

"I can do that, Del. You have the church to worry about."

A smile no longer graced his face. He got that cold, steely look that frightened her so. "I keep all our books. I'll be keeping these, too. I'm the man—that's my job."

Connie Jo wanted to argue, but the customers and the other stylists were right there and while perhaps Del had no problem with public scenes, Connie Jo had been raised to keep her dirty laundry private. And so, at the end of the day, he scooped up all the money, placed it into a bank bag, and that was that.

He pushed the receptionist to take in as many customers as possible, as soon as possible, even if it meant shortening the time slots for each visit. "If the girls know someone's waiting, they'll work faster. If you get them in today, there's less chance they'll go somewhere else. If people have to wait once they're here, they'll say to themselves, 'This place must be hot. Look at how busy it is. I never had to wait this long before. They took me right away.'"

It all sounded good—perhaps a little coldhearted, but maybe this was what Del brought to the situation. Connie Jo was softhearted, not a tough negotiator at all. Del could be downright mean when he wanted to be, and he wanted to be mean quite often.

The second day of business went much like the first, although by the end of the week the receptionist quit or was fired, depending upon whose story was to be believed. On one hand, Del took almost gleeful pleasure in bragging about how he had bagged her, exclaiming, "The first thing you do when you take over a business is fire someone. That sets the tone. Lets people know you mean business and you aren't to be crossed."

On the other hand, privately, he explained to Connie

Jo that he forced a resignation from the woman so that she wouldn't have a claim to unemployment. "Savin' you money right off the bat, I am," he said proudly.

"But Del, now I have to hire a new receptionist," said Connie Jo.

"I'll do it. Receptionist handles the money and no one but family should handle the money. People will rob you blind."

"But what about the church?"

Reverend Delbert Mobley resigned from Second Baptist Bible Church of Gainesville the very next day.

# Chapter Twenty-Four

It was a new life now, no longer a life of being a preacher's wife nor, for Del, a life of being a preacher. Connie Jo Mobley worked and went to school, getting her license in cosmetology in a year and a half of working part time and going to school part time. It was exhausting, but now she had a sense of accomplishment and independence.

As Del said, "Once you get your own license, you can hire and fire as you please. You won't owe anything to any of these other women." But Connie Jo liked the other stylists and had no desire to fire anybody. They all were good and they all carried their weight. If there was ever a dynamic tension, it was between Del Mobley and everyone else, including Connie Jo. He sat near the front door, reading a newspaper or watching the small television set he placed there. Other times he left for a while, doing God knew what, and a patina of calm came over the shop as if the big, bad wolf had gone at least for a time.

For as much as she enjoyed working the shop, she was chagrined to discover what Del's plot had to have been all along. He really didn't work anymore. He sat on his behind and took in money, but a monkey could have done that. No, he was simply a money-receiving machine and once that money hit his hand, Connie Jo never saw it again.

"How'd we do this month?" she'd ask.

"Fine," and that would be the end of the conversation. If she pried beyond that, Del would get his bulldog on, sometimes smacking her in the face. Once he even did it in the shop, while one customer was there as well as three other haircutters. Connie Jo was so mortified but wondered afterwards whether it was more of a warning shot, a way of pushing against her internal sense of embarrassment and public propriety. She'd be more frightened of him, less apt to question him or anything he did for fear he'd not only hurt her but publicly humiliate her as well.

Still, the shop must have been doing pretty well because Del continued to buy toys for himself—a luxury sedan, a new pickup truck, cameras, video equipment, TVs and VCRs. He seemed happy, yet in the shallowest of ways. Money made him happy. He no longer even attended church, whereas Connie Jo had to find a new parish, as she was far too embarrassed to attend services at Second Baptist, and she went every Sunday with the boys. This was the only time she was ever out of Del's sight, except for when he went on his personal shopping trips when he got bored at the beauty shop.

Del continued to dominate the telephone, only this time it extended to the phone at the shop. *Strange,* Connie Jo thought. When they were at home, only Del could answer the phone. At work, only Del could answer the phone. There were never any answering machines still. Connie Jo did get calls from her friends and family, but they all had to go through Del. That and the money.

Connie Jo not only had no idea how her business was doing, she had no idea of their personal finances. Del handled everything. Another woman might have been happy with this, having a big, strong man taking care of her, but Connie Jo had grown to be suspicious. He really wasn't taking care of her because again, all that they had was really hers. She was now the sole wage earner and she could only wonder what had happened to her savings as well as what was happening on an ongoing basis with the checks she got through the mail each month, courtesy of Ben's untimely demise.

Yet, there seemed little she could do. Del smacked her around at least once every two weeks or so. Maybe once every two months or so, the beatings were so bad that she was sincerely hurt and bruised. At least once, one of her employees at the shop asked her about a black eye she had, trying to gain her confidence, saying to Connie Jo, "Look, we all know how he treats you. We know that's how you got that thing on your face. No man should be able to get away with that. If you need a witness or someone to take you in or take you to the police, I'll be there for you. He doesn't scare me. Besides, my husband Earl would knock his block off if I asked him to."

But Connie Jo did what most abused women do. She denied it, claiming to have stepped on a garden rake—silly her.

Occasionally, while she was cutting hair, Connie Jo would look over at Del when he was engrossed in his little television. *Why is he like this? He has a gift. Why does he just toss it away and sit here all day long, watching over me and taking my hard-earned money like a pimp of some sort? Where is his pride? What could have damaged him so that he would go on throughout his life being his own worst enemy?*

The revelation of Del's self-destructive behavior accumulated as she managed bits and pieces of stealth conversations with her beloved brother, Rusty, who still preached in a church in St. Augustine. She could only listen, as Del always sat close by whenever Rusty called.

"I've come to find that that man's a living legend, but only in the worst way, sis. He's crashed and burned through a dozen churches all throughout the South. Everybody's heard of him by now. He gives a great sermon, but outside of that, some think he's pure evil. Have you seen that side of him? Has he ever hurt you? I swear, if I hear of him laying one hand on a hair of your head, I'll kill him. God forgive me, I will."

"Everything is fine," she would reply, cautiously watching Del watching her. "Everything is fine."

"Here, I got myself some coffee. Thought I'd get you a cup while I was at it." Del smiled as he handed it to Connie Jo, who was waiting for her next customer to finish getting shampooed. She smiled as she sipped. Del ran little errands like this all the time, such a comedown from his days of holding a throng in his hand as he preached the gospel, yet Connie Jo was thankful for any little displays of affection she received from him.

Just as the client slipped into Connie Jo's chair at her station, Connie Jo suddenly buckled as if she'd been shot. Burning pain shot through her stomach—a hot, fiery brick about to explode inside of her. Her legs felt the fire as well. When she doubled over and looked, she did not recognize them, all grotesquely ballooned out from the knee down. She slithered down, down, down, feeling like she was about to lose consciousness and throw up. She screamed, "Del! Del! Help me!"

Del walked over and helped her back to her feet. "C'mon now. You're alright. Probably just had coffee on an empty stomach. I'll go next door for a cookie or something."

"No, Del…I feel like I'm gonna die," she replied.

"Nonsense. C'mon, Charlotte here is ready for her cut. You shouldn't keep the customers waiting."

But even the customers knew something was drastically wrong. "I think you should take her to the hospital. She don't look right," said Charlotte, the woman standing nearby, her hair all wet, waiting with her black-plastic smock around her torso.

"Now, now honey, you just sit here. It'll only be a minute. I'll go get that cookie. Maybe a muffin," said Del as he turned to leave.

By the time he returned, Connie Jo was sprawled out on the floor, near unconsciousness, vomit all around her, her breathing strained and shallow. The other women in the salon looked at Del Mobley like he was some sort of monster. "We're calling nine-one-one. We think she's gonna die."

"Alright, alright. Put that phone down. I'll put her in the truck and take her to the doctor. I'm sure he'll find there's nothing serious at all wrong." With that, Del scooped her up. Unable to stand or walk on her own, he soon had her cradled like a baby in his large arms.

At the doctor's office, Connie Jo got poked and prodded while she threw up a few more times. She ingested clear fluids and became a bit more cognizant, but still remained the picture of gastronomical agony.

"Have you been having any marital problems?" the doctor asked. Connie Jo rolled her eyes over towards Del, who had a determined look on his face—not entirely angry, but with the strength and the wherewithal to be as mean and ornery as ever.

"No, no problems," she answered, knowing she could not say a word or express negativity while Del was in the room.

"I think you may be getting an ulcer. Maybe gallstones. I'll run a few tests and give you something for your stomach. I think you'll be fine."

"Thank you, Doc. I owe you," said Del, as he tried to make light of the entire situation and bum rush Connie Jo out the door.

Once they were back in the car, Connie Jo moaned, "Del, this is bad. This is the worst I ever felt in my entire life. Please don't make me go back to work. I can't possibly stand."

Del huffed and puffed, finally acquiescing to bringing her home. "Doctor said everything's gonna be alright. You're just acting like a drama queen."

"I think that doctor's a quack. I'm telling you, Del, this is serious. I've been sick plenty of times in my life, but I ain't never felt anything like this before. This is what death must feel like."

Once they got home, Del plopped down beside her on the bed. Connie Jo actually feared he'd start undressing and fooling around with her. He did strange things like that, as if somehow when she was in her weakest states, he wanted her the most. It was a sick trait, something that sickened her as much as his penchant for pornography.

She had begun to abhor sex with this man. She knew it wasn't right, but she had such a hard time getting him to act nice and truly be loving when they were together. Still, as in so many other aspects of their life, she wondered to herself whether some of it was her own fault. Del had that power over her, the ability to make her question everything about herself, to make her feel guilty when things were bad between them. She'd been in this vulnerable state ever since Ben had died. Del had caught her at a low point, a time when she was still blaming herself for that.

"Now the shop's hopping with business and we're here doing nothing," Del said, miffed.

"You can go back if you want. If I take a turn for the worse, I can call an ambulance."

"No, no, I'll stay here. If they rob us blind, they rob us blind. Maybe that will make you more of a soldier and less of a baby the next time you get sick," he said. With that, Connie Jo tried to roll over and away from him, feeling about as sick and as low as one can possibly imagine.

## Chapter Twenty-Five

With the passage of time, Connie Jo began to improve ever so slightly. No one seemed to know for sure whether it was a correct prognosis from her doctor or merely if whatever it was that she had had simply passed. She went back to work but every few weeks or so, an identical attack would occur. Each time, Del would act as though she were being a bother and a chronic complainer, despite the fact that she would often lose consciousness and spew vomit and diarrhea everywhere. He would drive her home or to the local family physician, who would give her something for ulcers or, perhaps, explore some other possible cause for her repetitive dilemma, and then after a few days of bed rest she would be well enough to go back to work again.

"Del, I'm dying. I know I am. It's cancer. I know it," she said, her eyes full of tears.

"Oh, hush now. You got something else going on and it can't be as bad as cancer. You'll be fine," said Del as he stood by her bedside.

"But look at all these other symptoms. Why are my extremities blowing up like balloons?"

"You're on your feet all day long at work," he replied.

"Then why don't the other girls look like this? That makes no sense, Del. And the discoloration. If I get any deeper a shade of purple, I'm going to look like an eggplant!"

On a few occasions, her doctor told her to go to the local hospital for tests but nothing of great consequence turned up. Once, they found gallstones and even operated to remove her gall bladder, but after the fact it appeared that the organ was fine and need not have been removed. Weakened overall, her recovery from the surgery was slow and uncomfortable.

One summer morning as she lay in bed, far too sick and in pain to go in to work again, Del made her some breakfast. "Well, here I go again, into town, running what's supposed to be *your* business," he harrumphed.

All she could do was turn her head away slightly. He didn't care. He truly did not care how badly she felt. This was what slow and painful death felt like, she was sure of it, and yet her own husband was only marginally tolerant of her, let alone concerned for her future and well-being. Instead, he trudged off to collect money—*her* money from her business begun with her money.

Shortly after he left, Connie Jo felt a pain like a wallop to the gut. She literally bolted upright, grabbing her stomach along the way. It felt like there was a bomb in her abdomen, doubling her over, twisting and flaming like a rocket caught in a space too small for it to fly. Her head spun. She was still in bed, yet the room was moving like a carousel. Everything around her turned to liquid. Everything inside of her poured out, exploding out of every orifice. Sweat, vomit and everything else pooled around her and still, it kept coming.

"Help," she cried feebly, but there was no one there. B.J. and Gabe were playing over at the home of a friendly neighbor who had kids around their same ages. Del was gone.

She reached for the phone by the bed and began to dial, not sure she could even hit 9-1-1 without messing up as her head spun 'round and 'round. She tried to punch in the numbers; she *might* have punched in the numbers, she couldn't even be sure. Now all she could do was wait. And wait. River-like torrents rushed through her ears. She wondered if she would even be able to hear anyone answering the phone from the other end of the line. Nothing. She heard nothing. Would she be able to keep conscious long enough to tell the operator where she was, who she was and what she wanted? She tried to concentrate, to take her mind off of the worst pain she'd ever felt, so she could recite her vitals to the operator.

No one was there. She was lucid; she swore she was, but there was no ringing, no operator, no message, no nothing. She hung up and tried again. This time, she attempted to focus from the moment she began the dialing, an activity that suddenly became as labored as trying to run a footrace while 100 feet under water.

There was no dial tone. With her last bit of strength, she hung up and tried again. For a third time, she picked up the phone. No tone. Dead phone.

This was the last thing Connie Jo Mobley remembered. What she learned later was that her eldest son, B.J., came home early, unannounced, to look for a piece of play equipment. He shouted for her and heard no response. Tentatively, he climbed the stairs, continuing to shout, "Momma! Momma!" But no Momma answered.

When he found his mother lying in bed, covered in a liquid stench of her own making, he at first thought she was dead. Ignoring the rancidness that enveloped the room, he ran over to her, grabbing her, trying to wake her out of her Snow White sleep. Her mouth opened and she gasped. To his young, untrained eye, this meant life, although it could have just as easily been nothing more than an autonomic response, like air being squeezed out of a plastic sandwich bag. Still, encouraged, he, too, grabbed the phone and found the same thing—dead nothingness.

Releasing his mother, he ran around the house like a crazy boy, wisely looking for all of the phones. He remembered this happening once before—a phone slightly ajar and off the hook in one room, deadening all the other phones.

He didn't have to look too hard this time. Instead of finding a similar accident, he went into the den and found a phone with no hand unit resting upon it at all. He traced the cord and found the handset purposely shoved inside a drawer underneath the end table upon which it rested. The drawer was shut. This was no accident.

A few minutes later, what had been a perfectly quiet house was abuzz with activity. Police, paramedics, and ambulance drivers set about getting Connie Jo out of the house and off to a hospital. That was exactly when Del Mobley entered.

"What the hell is going on here?" he demanded. B.J., having reattached the phone, had called 9-1-1 and followed up by placing a call to Del at the beauty shop. To B.J.'s ear, Del had not been pleased, and luckily for the mother and child, B.J. had called emergency services first rather than Del, because he, as he had been doing all along, pooh-poohed the entire situation. "She'll be fine. Go out and play. I'll drive in and see what she needs."

But now Del stood amidst the cacophony and he did not like it one bit. "This is my house. What're y'all doing in here?"

"Your wife is very sick. We're bringing her to the hospital," answered one of the emergency personnel.

But instead of acting shocked and concerned about his wife's condition, he protested, "That ain't necessary. She's been sick a while now. It's just a flu or something. Y'all can go away now, don't be making a fuss. We can't afford this."

But no one was listening to him and this did not sit well with Del Mobley, who was used to everyone jumping when he barked. Realizing he was not being obeyed, he looked around for young B.J. "Boy, what the hell is goin' on?"

"Sir, I called nine one one. That's what they taught us to do in school. Momma didn't seem to be breathing. I thought she might be dead or dyin'," he said, his eyes finally welling up with tears as he spoke.

Del Mobley's face reddened like a kettle about to whistle, then he smacked the boy across the face. "Boy, don't you *ever* bring people into my house again! This is *my* house! These people are marching through here like it's a public square, like they're some army taking over my place."

"But Momma—"

Del cut him off by smacking him again. This time B.J. turned his head away and cried, unable to complete his thought. A paramedic with one foot out the door and one foot in, wheeling Connie Jo out on a gurney, looked up and appeared as if he might intervene were Del to take just one more strike at the lad but, seeing that did not occur, merely gave the man a disgusted, confused and disapproving look and continued about his business in silence. A policeman nearby, though, did not.

"You the man of the house?" he asked Del as he approached.

"Yes."

"Come over here a minute, I want to talk to you," he said as he firmly grabbed Del by the upper arm and moved him away from B.J.

"But my wife is going away in that ambulance. I have to be with her," Del protested.

"I'll drive you right behind it. You won't miss anything. Just come on over here," he said as he finally got Del into a private corner. There, he dropped his voice a bit. "What are you doin'? I saw you hit that boy. That boy saved your wife's life. I don't know yet what her trouble is but those paramedics worked on her and she's in a terrible way. And if it's a flu, then it's the worst damn flu I ever saw in my life. Don't let me ever see you hitting on that boy again or I'll run you in for domestic violence. Are we clear?"

Del dropped his chin, then raised it back up again, staring the cop right in the face like a boxer facing down his next opponent, but he said nothing.

"I said, *are we clear?*" the policeman said again, this time leaning forward so that he was close enough to Del to kiss him, spitting out his words, almost daring him to start trouble.

Del continued to stare, then slowly and silently dropped his eyes in acknowledgement. Now the policeman's voice changed to a whisper. "What is the matter with you, man? Your wife is sick and you show her no concern. All you do is yell at her boy. Do you do this all the time? Is this how you treat your family?"

Del wasn't answering. Finally, the cop backed off.

# Chapter Twenty-Six

Connie Jo Mobley looked more like a Frankenstein monster than a pretty, young woman. Tubes were stuck in her every which way. Her skin varied from pale to purple, no tone looking in any way attractive. She was alive and breathing, even regaining consciousness from time to time, but not really able to speak coherently.

Del Mobley hovered around her in her hospital room, looking more like a man in a police holding pen awaiting his lawyer than a truly concerned husband. BJ sat in a corner quietly, hoping Del would not begin hitting him again. B.J. had begun to do this a lot. He had come to sincerely fear the man, fear him more than any other emotion he could muster towards him. Gabe, his kid brother, didn't seem to feel quite the same. It could have been personalities or age, but more likely it was because Del clearly favored the younger boy.

It could have been something as simple as his name. Del Mobley prided himself outwardly for being the father—not stepfather, but father, as he put it—of two boys, but B.J.'s name always came off his tongue like a piece of rotten meat. And nothing made him angrier than when Connie Jo called the boy by his full name—Benjamin or Ben Junior. Ben was the name of some man who'd had his wife before he had, and that did not rest well with him, nor did the fact that B.J.'s name led to all sorts of questions that brought out the fact that Del was not his father.

But Gabriel, that was his child, even though he wasn't. Gabe hardly remembered his father at all by this time, a fact that upset Connie Jo terribly but pleased Del to no end. That one, Gabe, was now his, at least in Del's mind.

The door to the room opened and in sprang nearly all of the Roberts clan—Brother Rusty followed by wives, sisters and Connie Jo's parents, along with young Gabe. Del's head snapped again in the direction of B.J. "You called all them, too?" he asked accusatorially.

B.J. raised his head slightly, perhaps emboldened by the presence of his mother's family—*his* family. "Momma told me to call Uncle Rusty if things ever got bad."

"Boy, you…"

But by then all of Connie Jo's people were smothering her with love, surrounding her bed, and no one was listening or paying any attention at all to Del Mobley, which again incensed him. He resigned himself to staring out the window, ignoring them as they ignored him.

Groggily, Connie Jo tried to speak despite the tube down her throat and another one up her nose. It was nearly impossible to hear her or understand her, but somehow she squeaked, "I can't move my legs, my arms. I hurt so bad."

Her sisters and her sister-in-law began crying and some even started to pray. Rusty held her and comforted her. He looked around and caught Del's eye, but his look was not an approving one. Without a word directly to him, he said to the room, "I'm going out to speak to the doctors," and he left without looking for Del's approval or response. On his way out, he put his hand around B.J.'s shoulder. "You want to come with me, Junior? I could use a man's help." Del seethed.

When they returned, Rusty walked over to Del just like the policeman had and said, "You and me, we gotta talk." For the second time in a day, a strong man who wasn't afraid of him pulled Del Mobley out of a room.

"What kind of man are you?"

"Whut?" asked Del.

"You heard me. My sister looks like death warmed over in there and we haven't been called? What have you been doing?"

"I've been taking care of her. When she doesn't feel good I bring her to the doctor. What else do you expect me to do?" Del replied.

Rusty Roberts glared at Del. "Have you gotten a good

diagnosis? Have you gotten a second opinion? Is anything they're doing for her here making her better?"

Del could hardly do much more than shrug his shoulders.

"I don't know what's worse—you or these quack doctors in this backwoods hospital. I just made a call. They're bringing in a helicopter to take my sister to Flagler Hospital in St. Augustine. It's the finest hospital in the state."

"But we live here. This is our local hospital," said Del.

Like the cop, Rusty brought his face even closer to Del's. "You're no longer in charge. I am. You had your chance and you blew it. My sister's boy finally told me how you've been treating her and him—hitting them and smacking them around. And now this. Well let me tell you something, Brother. When this is through, I might just take you outside and give you a lesson you'll never forget. Hitting women and children. What kind of man are you?"

Del suddenly grew calmer. "You threatening me?"

Rusty didn't take the bait. "When this is over, I'm advising my sister to divorce your sorry self for her own sake as well as for my nephews—that I can promise you. *That ain't a threat.*" With that, he turned away and went down the corridor.

Del Mobley called after him, but Rusty paid him no attention, not even turning around. "She's my wife, not yours. And they're my boys."

A few minutes later, some hospital people came to the

room with forms and such. "The helicopter is here to take your wife to Flagler, Mr. Mobley."

"That's *Reverend* Mobley. I didn't call no helicopter. My wife is afraid to fly. And I never requested she be moved to some other hospital. I ain't signing anything."

Folks looked from side to side at one another. Rusty Roberts was no longer in sight. "But the helicopter is here, sir."

Del looked around to make sure Rusty wasn't rounding the bend. "Send it away."

---

Not long thereafter, Rusty Roberts returned to the hospital room to comfort his sister. He said nothing to Del Mobley, nor did Del say anything to him. It seemed as if the room were divided between two countries—Del alone on one side, and the Robertses on the other.

After a few hours, Rusty left the room for a bit and then returned again. This time, he entered in a furious rage, rushing over to Del and grabbing him by the collar. "You sent the helicopter away?"

Del pushed back against him, but Rusty's grip was strong. "She doesn't need it," he replied.

Rusty stopped wrestling with Del but kept him pinned up near a standing lamp in the corner of the room. Everyone else turned to face the action, but Del and Rusty were in a world of their own, oblivious to them all. "You don't want her to get well, do you? You had something to do with this. You want her to die, don't you?"

"You're crazy, you know that?" Del said, still immobile and vulnerable, his head stretched back.

"Kelly Sue, call the nurse in. Tell her I have to talk to her." Rusty never let his grip on Del Mobley go.

"You gonna let me go, or am I gonna stay here like this for the rest of my life? I could sue you for assault and terroristic threats, you know that."

But Rusty did not budge. "When that nurse comes back in here, I'm telling them to bring back that helicopter. And I don't want to hear one peep out of you. If you say so much as one word against it, I will kill you, I swear to the Lord I will, 'cause I'm beginning to think this is all part of a bigger thing, you understand that? Not one damn word."

The nurse returned and Rusty finally allowed Del to straighten himself up. She brought in an administrator. "I'm sorry, Reverend Roberts, but we can't get that helicopter back here. They don't stand for any nonsense. The best I can do is get you an ambulance."

"Then get it. I want my sister safely transported out of here. And if there's any papers to sign, bring them here right now."

The administrator looked over at Del. "I'm sorry, but the husband is right over there and he has legal standing."

Rusty returned his glare to Del who, for his part, seemed to be trying to compose himself in such a way that he would look like the sanest, calmest man in the room. Rusty wasn't going to fall into that trap. "Can you remove that tube from my sister's throat so she can talk? Can you?"

"Yes, I think we can, for a bit."

"Fine, then she'll decide for herself," said Rusty as he moved over towards her. Slowly, the tube was pulled out and Connie Jo choked and coughed weakly. "Connie. Connie. Can you understand me? You're not getting better here. I want to take you to a good hospital around by me. I want a second opinion for you, honey. We're gonna take an ambulance there. It won't take all that long and I'll ride with you to keep you company."

"He's coercing her!" said Del Mobley. "She's not got her wits about her. He could get her to agree to just about anything in the state she's in."

Rusty turned to Del again. "Funny. When it suits you, you claim she's doin' just fine. Now she's incapable of thinking for herself. Which one is it, Del? Which one gets you whatever it is you want?"

"Rusty," Connie Jo whispered, for that was all she could do. "I want to go with you. Whatever you think is best."

"Coerced," Del repeated.

Rusty turned to the administrator. "Do me a favor—while she's signing this, you got somebody here can write up a durable power of attorney?"

"He's coercing her again," Del bellowed from across the room.

"Yes, we can do that," the administrator replied.

"You have any reason to believe, in your medical opinion, that my sister is not in her right mind? That she can't make her own decisions right now? When I ask her if she wants to go to this other facility, do you think she has no free will?"

"She's in bad shape, but she seems to be of sound mind. I can bring a staff psychiatrist down to make a formal determination if you desire. That would cover you legally."

"Do it. And get that ambulance revved up and ready to go. Nothing personal—I appreciate all you people have done for my sister. But I'm quarterbacking this team now 'cause my only interest is her well-being, nothing more."

The administrator, who had been talking to the doctors and nurses throughout the day, looked towards Del Mobley, then back again at Rusty, "I can see that, Reverend. We'll set you up."

Throughout the signing of the paper, Del kept loudly expressing his disproval yet tried to remain calm, or at least looking calm. "They're all crazy. They're making a mountain out of a molehill. Now they're trying to take away my rights as a husband and father. That ain't right. I know what's best for my wife and that's to stay here with me." But it was having the opposite effect and after a while, no one paid him any mind. Rusty was doing an even better job of staying calm and focused, taking care of business.

"Next he'll be coercing her to cut me out of her will, putting hisself in it."

Rusty paused for a second, then responded, "Thanks for

the idea, Del. I'll just stick to the part about cutting you out, though. I don't want or need a dime of my sister's money, or that of her first husband, the one who loved her."

That one got Del Mobley's goat and he rushed across the room as if to rumble with Rusty, but the entire Roberts family, most of them women, stood up in a cordon around him, daring him to strike out at all of them at once.

A man entered the room. "The ambulance is here."

"I'll be riding with her. I'm her husband," said Del.

"Like hell you will," said Rusty. "You're on notice from here on in. I'll be watching you."

# Chapter Twenty-Seven

"Tell me more about all this then," Rusty Roberts said to his sister once they were ensconced in her new hospital room in St. Augustine. She was resting a little easier, although the battery of endless tests they were giving her was taking a toll. Sometimes the cure is worse than the malady.

"Rusty, I just don't know. I never had any stomach problems before. But I haven't ever felt anything like this before. My hands and my legs—I can't work them, but I still feel a ton of pain in them—worse pain than I ever felt in my life. And look at me, look all over at me. No ulcer is gonna make a person look like this and be in this kind of pain and paralysis. It's cancer, I'm telling you, it's cancer. I have no other explanation."

"Well, sis, they don't know. They've been poking and prodding but they haven't turned up any cancer yet." Rusty held her hand, something she could hardly ever remember him doing. They were close, but he wasn't the type to be getting all huggy and kissy with her. She'd never seen him cry.

"Rusty, you'd tell me if it was cancer, wouldn't you? I know I'm in bad shape, but it's worse if I lie here wondering what's wrong with me than if you tell me the bad news. You know how the imagination is. We tend to think things are worse than they are and unless you are truthful with me, I'll only think the worst."

Connie Jo seemed in for the long haul. Parishioners from her home church in rural Alabama, her church in Montgomery, and her church in Gainesville all came to visit her once word spread that she was gravely ill. Folks would pray over her, hold her hand and ask what they could do for her.

Del Mobley was there most all of the time as well. He and Rusty clashed constantly, but Del seemed to visibly cower whenever Rusty stepped into the room. In Rusty, he had met his match, and he didn't like it one bit. Rusty, for his part, couldn't stand the man and wasn't afraid to let him know it. He knew better than to drone on and on to Connie Jo about it, though. She had her hands full just trying to hang on and get better. The last thing Rusty wanted to do was upset her.

All three parishes set up funds to help with Connie Jo Mobley's medical care. When people would stop by, they would hand Del Mobley envelopes full of cash, or else checks made out to Connie Jo. In either case, he would slip off to the bank and nothing more was made of it. "You're such a loving husband, Brother Del, staying at this poor sweetheart's side day and night. God bless the two of you." Those were the sentiments that kept Del buoyant until the next time Rusty Roberts would come and douse his high-and-pious opinion of himself.

Connie Jo seemed to never be alone, and this was good. Del made a few trips back to Gainesville for this and that, most likely to collect money from the beauty shop. Rusty was by early every day for at least an hour or two.

One day, a face Connie Jo had not seen in years poked her head in. "Oh, my Lord, Connie Jo," Exa Shirey gasped. She slapped her hand across her own mouth once she said it, but Connie Jo was wide awake at the time and heard it loud and clear.

"Yes, I know. I suppose you could say I'm not ready for my close up, if you know what I mean." Connie Jo knew how she looked and as much as it pained her, she could no longer afford to be vain about it.

"Oh, Connie Jo, I am so sorry. I'm sorry for everything. I'm sorry we've lost touch and that we let things come between us."

"Come on over here. I'd rather you be here than feel you had to stay away," Connie Jo replied, motioning her over to the bed. There, they chatted, and after a while, Connie Jo started to doze and Exa began to pray out loud over her.

"If you have the faith, get up and walk."

"Exa, I can't," Connie Jo said groggily.

"You must. You must pray now and you must feel the strength of the Lord deep inside of you."

Connie Jo hadn't the strength to explain or even to talk much more. Her face told all. Something was direly wrong, no one knew what it was, and there was nothing she could do about it. All she could do was lie there, helpless and confused.

Exa kept praying over her until finally she said, "You mustn't have the faith no more."

It was perhaps the cruelest thing Connie Jo had ever heard, crueler still in that she wondered if there was at least an ounce of truth to it. She hated Del Mobley at times. When Exa and church people like her came to visit her, she felt mixed emotions, not the least of which was shame. Del had made her embarrassed to be around many of these people. He had burned bridges in Montgomery and bridges in Gainesville. Yes, some still believed in him as a man of God, but there were many others in those parishes who no longer did.

Which group was right? At times she was moved to tears at the Christian patronage of the ones who came to see her, while at other times she only looked upon them as fools who had no idea how evil Del Mobley could be, especially to her.

And what did that say about her? She was still married to the man. When she was home, she shared a bed with him. Even up to the day that he gave his last sermon in Gainesville, she felt enthralled by the sound of his voice when he summoned up the spirit. But that spell only lasted so long on her. Once he stopped preaching, not simply as an occupation but even when he stopped praising the Lord during services, she looked at him and felt resentment and hatred sometimes, reflecting upon how he beat her, berated her, took from her and mistreated her sons. What kind of hypocrite was he, this liar and charlatan?

Yet it was not until this very moment that she wondered the same about herself. What was God doing to her? Had He come to understand the bad things she felt towards her husband? Was this all God's punishment? If Del was a man of God and now she doubted Del, had she also begun to lose her faith in God? Was that why she was being torn up inside, why she could no longer walk?

*

Del came back to the hospital after a short trip back to Gainesville. Rusty was in Connie Jo's room. They exchanged sneers.

"Del, did you remember to bring me my extra nightgown and my sleepy socks? I'm here so long, I need to feel fresh. I can't be living in these same clothes all the time."

"No, I forgot," Del replied, annoyed. Then, looking at the disapproving Rusty, he added, "Sorry." Del often slept on a cot in Connie Jo's hospital room, and the boys were staying at Rusty's house while their mother was in the hospital in St. Augustine.

"Tell you what, sis. I'm off tomorrow. How's about I run

by your house and pick you up what you need? I'd be glad to help."

"There's no need for that. She's my wife. I'll bring her things if she wants," said Del.

"Well, looks like you've been falling down on the job. I'll do it. Sis, you got an extra key?"

"Hey now," said Del, "That's my house you're talking about. You don't be going into my house without me there."

Rusty Roberts looked Del Mobley square in the eye. "It's my sister's house, too. And if I got it right, she put down the down payment and she's the only one bringing in an income, so she's the only one paying the mortgage. The way I see it, it's more her house than yours."

"Just you wait a minute," Del huffed. "She ain't making no living lying here in a hospital bed. I'm paying the mortgage now."

"Oh, so now you're cutting people's hair, I see. Doin' pedicures, too?" Rusty tweaked.

"You don't go into my house without me there. I'm, telling you that, right here, right now."

"Stop it, both of you," said Connie Jo. "Del, I trust Rusty with my life. What's the big deal if he drops by the house and got me a few things?"

"Yeah, Del, what's the problem?" Rusty repeated. "You got something to hide?"

Del looked like he would explode, but after a few seconds the blood ran away from the front of his face and he calmed down his demeanor. "Fine, then. Maybe you can take the boy with you when you go. He can pick up some things for him and his brother while you're at it." Del always called B.J. "the boy," while he took more to calling Gabe "my son." He was dividing and conquering and it saddened Connie Jo so.

"Fine. I'll probably be there around two o'clock. If you think of anything else you need, sis, just let me know before I leave town."

"Is my momma gonna die?"

Rusty Roberts hated the question because he sincerely did not know the answer. The boy had been through so much in his young life already, it seemed cruel that such concerns would trouble his head. Connie Jo wasn't getting better and, in fact, from time to time she would have additional attacks, right there in the hospital—flare-ups where she would scream in agony, her eyes rolling back into her head, vomiting all over the place. Why would she seem to be getting better, then turn again for the worse?

At one point they tried "washing her blood" or some such thing. They transfused all the blood she had and "rinsed" it with a machine of some sort, then put it back into her. That seemed to work best; she really perked up after that treatment, But then, two days later, it was as if it had never happened. It befuddled the doctors and it more than befuddled Rusty, a nonmedical man.

"Listen, young man, your sister loves you with all her

heart. I know she's glad you're thinking of her, but worrying about her won't make her any better. It may even make her worse. We shouldn't be worrying her by worry *about* her. I just want you to know two things: God is watching down over all of us—your momma, your brother, you, me. The second thing is that I'm watching over the three of you also. I want you to know I'm here for you. You can come to me for anything." He brought his arm around B.J. to hug him. As he raised his arm, out of the corner of his eye it seemed like the boy flinched a little.

"Ben Junior, does Del hit you?"

B.J. slumped down in his car seat, unsure of how to answer. The question made him clearly uncomfortable. "Sometimes," he almost whispered.

Part of Rusty wanted to whip the car around, head back to St. Augustine and beat the living heck out of Del Mobley. But perhaps that's what the boy feared. He tried to put himself in the kid's shoes. What was the one thing a kid who'd been hit by an adult wanted? Peace. He wanted peace and serenity and no more hitting. That was a good thing—good for then, at least.

What Rusty feared was that as time went on, the boy would grow to be a man and his search for peace would be abandoned, replaced by the need for revenge, and if Del wasn't there for him to dole it out on him, he'd instead grow up to start beating on his own wife and kids, never really understanding why he felt the need to do so. He'd become just like the monster who beat on him. That's the patterns

Rusty had seen in his ministering. It was so, so very wrong, but it went on all the time and it was a crying shame. And so he calmed himself and gave the boy some peace. He held B.J.'s shoulder gently as he drove, letting this skittish boy know what it was like to have a decent, kind man somewhere in his life.

Rusty and BJ rolled up towards the Mobley residence. The first thing Rusty did once he parked was go to the mailbox to see if there was anything in there. Empty. Strange. Everybody got at least a piece or two of junk mail every day. How long had it been since Del had last been here? He tried to recount.

As he walked up the driveway towards the front door, he thought to look down at his feet for the daily newspaper. No paper. Odd again. He thought they got the paper delivered there every day. Connie Jo had mentioned how much she liked to begin her day by reading the local paper. Maybe Del had called to stop it. Same too with the mail. Yeah, that made sense.

No sooner had Rusty taken the key out of the door and begun to open it than he smelled it. "Gas!" he shouted out of habit. B.J. was right behind him. "B.J., run back into my car. Go on now!" The boy did as he was told.

Part of Rusty wanted to run out, too, but he thought it might be smart if he could take a step or two inside to see if the cause of the problem was something obvious and if he could fix it. Maybe an unlit burner on top of the stove was still on. If he could switch if off quickly and open all the doors and windows, he wouldn't have to make a big fuss about it with the fire department and gas company people.

He walked into the kitchen and checked the stove. Nothing was amiss. He looked around a bit more, but then he began to get scared. *This is nuts. I could get killed or keel over in here,* he thought as he made his way back from whence he came.

The last thing he saw as he neared the front door was a small, decorative end table. Upon it were the daily newspaper and a bunch of mail. *What the heck?* he thought to himself. He quickly grabbed the pile and walked out the door, leaving it open to vent the place while he figured he'd go out to his car to call the fire department.

Rusty Roberts was halfway up the driveway when the explosion occurred.

# Chapter Twenty-Eight

Rusty Roberts was as shook up as he had ever been in his life, but he was alive and relatively unhurt as he stayed near the scene, watching as firemen hosed down his sister's house. Fire was the least of it, though, as the house pretty much had exploded, leaving not much but frame and foundation.

Rusty wiped away at his dirty scrapes. He was given medical attention, but a trip to the hospital for X-rays did not seem necessary to him and so he backed off from the offer. The fire marshal asked him dozens of questions and he answered them all accurately and to the best of his abilities.

"It was the darndest thing, it really was," he kept saying, and he meant it, too. Never before had he felt so close to death himself and despite his faith, he was shaken up and scared. *I could have been in there. B.J. and I both could have been in there when it happened. I only beat it by a couple of seconds. God must surely been watching over me. Why was I such a fool not to run out the moment I smelled the gas? What am I, crazy?* he thought to himself. Rusty did not think of himself as a hero, far from it. He'd been reckless and for that he felt embarrassed.

As he spoke to the fire marshal, one of the firemen walked over. "I picked these up by the end of the driveway. They seem to be addressed to your house." The man did not know that Rusty was not the owner of the house. Rusty thanked him absentmindedly, though, recognizing it as the mail and newspaper he'd had in his hand as he'd left Connie Jo's home.

Mail. The day's newspaper. How in God's name could that have been inside the house? Rusty checked the date of the newspaper. Today. Connie Jo was in the hospital in St. Augustine. Del Mobley was supposed to be with her. If he had been here in Gainesville, why wouldn't he have waved Rusty off, telling him he needn't come by the house, that he was going to be there himself and could pick up the things for Connie Jo?

Rusty tossed it all around in his mind. Yes, Del had told him not to come at first, but that was more about being proprietary regarding Rusty being in his home. Once that was resolved, what then? It made no sense. Rusty wasn't driving all the way to Gainesville for his health; he was simply trying to do his sister a favor.

He tried keeping B.J. in his car and away from the tumult. The explosion had to have shaken the boy something terrible. The look of shock seemed to stay on his face for hours. Rusty kept checking in on him, assuaging his fears. The only good part of it all was that it seemed to take the boy's mind off of his sick mother.

As Rusty strolled back to the car to begin the long drive back to St. Augustine, he began shuffling through the mail, more out of habit than anything else. He felt just a little bit embarrassed, feeling he was looking into some other person's life that way. But that's what people habitually do when they have a fist full of mail—they page through it.

One piece of mail hit him. Very official looking. The Internal Revenue Service. Like every citizen, he got things from them from time to time, mostly blank forms and such. But this looked different. It looked like they really wanted it opened and answered right away.

He knew he shouldn't do it. He prayed on it during those few seconds before he actually did, but he had so very many concerns and suspicions about this Del Mobley character. He knew the man was beating his sister and his nephews. He'd discovered he'd been tossed out of more than a dozen churches across the South. Rusty even wondered if he had anything to do with his sister's poor health of late. And now this, this letter from the IRS, and the fact that it appeared quite clear that Del Mobley had been to this very house this very same day, beating him by, perhaps, a matter of hours, maybe less—beating him to it on a day when it exploded from a gas leak of some sort. Fishy. Mighty, mighty fishy.

Rusty opened the letter. Lots of bureaucratic legal jargon, but in the end, the bottom line was clear: "Dear Reverend Mobley. This is your final notice. Your employer withholding taxes, interest and penalties on Brodel Incorporated, d/b/a Connie Jo's Hair and Nail Salon, are $198,000 and have not been paid in nine quarters. This must be paid in full by August 1 or we shall begin legal proceedings. Please call us at…" And so on and so forth.

One hundred ninety-eight thousand dollars. Rusty Roberts had never seen such an amount of money all at one time in his life. His own house had not even cost that much, and he had a thirty-year mortgage on it. How on Earth could a man run up such debt? How did he expect to pay it? It would take him a lifetime to pay.

Unless…Unless…Rusty Roberts sat in his car, baffled. BJ.. sat quietly next to him. The boy was so emotionally tired that his eyes were half shut. Rusty bent over his steering wheel, trying to sort it all out.

*The man simply never paid taxes, that was the long and short of it. Those taxes had to be on all of their income, not just their own but on their employees' as well. Employers have to match some of what they take out of employees' salaries and they also have to pay to the government that which they take out for taxes. To accrue this large an amount, Del Mobley had to have just stuck it all in his pocket, every last dime, every last penny of profit, and every last nickel of withholding. Did Connie Jo know about this? No, she couldn't have. No way my sister could be so irresponsible. She'd never been like that. She* was more organized than all of us put together. And she never spent and splurged, never. Look at this…*

And Rusty looked in the direction of the house. It was too big; he'd always felt that. But Del had to put on a show all the time. He always…But there was no house there anymore. Gone, all gone.

*He must have blown up the house to pay the taxes. But wait…What about the mortgage? He had to have been carrying a mortgage. The mortgage company always gets their money first. The mortgage company always puts its name on the insurance policy. All Del would get in his pocket would be what little they'd have paid off and put down.*

Rusty tried to do the figuring in his head, but he dismissed it after a short time. He didn't know the cost of the house nor its belongings, all of which were gone now. But it didn't take a genius to figure out that Del Mobley would still come out short, and by quite a bit. And even if he gave whatever he had left over to the IRS, what would he and Connie Jo live on? Where on Earth would they even live?

He held the IRS letter in his hand as he stared and stared at the wreckage that was once a fine home. *I could have been killed in there. Me and B.J. Del knew we were coming here. I could have been dead, B.J. could have been dead, and Connie Jo…*

Yes, Connie Jo seemed to be barely hanging onto life. Del Mobley not only had to have had insurance on the house, he must have had life insurance on Connie Jo. He was probably also in Connie Jo's will, along with the boys.

But if Connie Jo was gone and B.J. was gone, that only left little Gabe. As for himself, there would be no money in that for Del Mobley, but he certainly would be getting a nagging nemesis out of the way.

Rusty Roberts prayed to God to remove these horrible thoughts from his head. The man was flawed, but he couldn't be a murderer, could he? He was a minister. He'd heard him preach and even he thought he seemed filled with the spirit. And his sister loved him despite all the problems she'd been having since she'd married him. There had to be something there, some ray of hope for Del Mobley's soul. He couldn't be a stone-cold murderer.

And then he thought, *This isn't the first home of his that has been destroyed suspiciously. There was that fishing cabin of his, too.* Rusty asked forgiveness of the Lord and mumbled to himself. "Lord, you gave us minds to think and arms to do, and we must do your works, even when the task seems disheartening."

He gunned his car back to St. Augustine.

# Chapter Twenty-Nine

Rusty burst into Connie Jo's hospital room. Del Mobley was there, as usual. It took all the strength he had not to race over and punch the man in the nose, but Rusty kept his lesser motivations in check. "Del, your house blew up. They think it was some sort of gas leak. I got a phone number for the fire marshal. He wants you to call him right away," he said as he handed Del a business card.

Del looked at him like he'd seen a ghost. "Yeah, okay, I'll call him." He pulled out his cell phone but Rusty stopped him. "Signs say no cell phones in the rooms. You could go down to the lobby. I'll stay with Connie Jo for you." It took a massive acting job for Rusty even to be civil to him.

"Okay, thanks," mumbled the dumbfounded Del.

As soon as he got out of sight, Rusty turned to his sister.

"My house blew up? Oh, my God, are you and B.J. alright? Did—"

But Rusty cut her off. "Listen, I gotta make this fast. We can chitchat more some other time. Connie Jo, do you have a will drawn up?"

Connie Jo's face became sallow. "Rusty, did they tell you I haven't long to live?"

"No, no, nothing like that. Just tell me, do you have a will?"

"Yes, yes of course I do. I got one the moment I had the children," she replied, still looking upset.

"Did you change it when you married Del? Is he in it?"

"Why, yes. I sort of didn't want to. I didn't ever see the point. I wanted everything to go to the boys, but he insisted if I didn't specify him in it, somebody else, or maybe the state or some such thing, could take the boys as well as the money. Why?"

"Connie Jo, I'm going to call a lawyer. I want you to change your will. I want you to take Del out of it. I know he's been hitting you and the boys. I suspect he set that fire on the fishing cabin for the insurance money. I think what happened to your house today was on purpose, and I even think he may have something to do with what's wrong with you."

"Oh, dear. Oh, no, Rusty, no. Del loves me. He tells me that all the time. He says he loves me and he'd die for me. He wouldn't do anything like this to me. How could you think such a thing?"

"God forgive me, but there are just too many things that when you add them all up, it don't look good. Listen, even if I'm wrong, there's no logic for him to be in your will. Leave everything to the boys. No government people are going to take money away from them…" And his voice trailed off.

"There's another thing," Rusty said, his pace slowing and his voice dropping. "Do you know anything about your owing money to the IRS?"

Connie Jo went silent. "Del takes care of everything now. I don't handle the money, he does." She sounded like a child about to be spanked—sad and embarrassed.

Rusty turned the IRS letter over to her. "You owe the IRS a hundred and ninety-eight thousand dollars."

Connie Jo read the letter in detail. Her eyes began to fill with tears. "Oh, God. Oh, my dear God."

"It's your life, sis, but I have to step up now and be strong for you—you *and* the boys. If I'm wrong about Del, what I'm suggesting you do with your will won't harm anything. Like you said, you want your money to go to the boys. That's all we're doing. I'm just strongly advising you to cut out the middleman. It's too much of a temptation."

"Temptation to do what?" Connie Jo asked, but then she quieted and without Rusty saying another word, she knew.

"I'm going out in the hall to call my lawyer and speak to the doctors. Colby and I will try to be here around the clock. I'll have Kelly Sue and Florence relieve us as well. We'll try to make it so you're hardly ever alone."

"Why?" Connie Jo cried. "I don't know what you're

suggesting." But her face belied her words. She could see how serious Rusty was, and it made her scared. Rusty was the best man she ever had known, and he had never jumped to bad conclusions before in his life.

There was a rustling of footsteps at the door and Rusty and Del switched places, Del coming back into Connie Jo's room and Rusty leaving. Rusty couldn't even bear to look Del in the eye as he brusquely rushed past him. The tension between them was palpable.

Del tried to pass it off as if he were the normal one and Rusty were the one acting all crazy and agitated towards him. "Geez, what's his problem? I'm the one whose house just got destroyed," he said as he got closer to Connie Jo.

Connie Jo also looked away from Del. "Are you alright, honey? How are you feeling now?" He sat next to her and gently patted her forehead, fixing a stray strand of hair.

Looking off into a faraway place, Connie Jo was able to muster up the courage to confront Del, for she knew if she actually looked into his eyes she would either lose her nerve or be persuaded by his tricky ways with words. "Do we owe money to the government?"

Del stopped caressing her face. "Everybody owes money to the government. Why?"

"A hundred and ninety-eight thousand dollars' worth?"

She could not see Del, for she was still afraid to look his way, but she could hear him quietly stutter and stammer, playing for time. "What are you talking about?"

Connie Jo made sure she spoke clearly, over-enunciating every syllable. "We owe the government one hundred and ninety-eight thousand dollars in back taxes. Why is that, and why did you hide it from me?"

Del rose to his feet. "Woman, you're crazy. We don't owe anything near that to nobody. What's gotten into you? Are you hallucinating or something?"

"Rusty has a copy of the bill. He got it from inside our house...before it blew up...mysteriously. Just like the cabin. I don't want to get into some stupid argument about whether he had a right to see it or not, that's not the point. But when he shows it to you and it says what it says, I'll be wanting an answer to these questions and more."

Never before had Connie Jo been so willing to directly confront Del Mobley. But there she was, in a hospital, surrounded by nurses, doctors and family. He couldn't hurt her there, she thought. Still, she spoke to him in dull, even tones, no strength for her to shout, and again, she did so while staring all the while at the wall, away from where Del stood. If he hit her then, she couldn't have cared less. She felt dead already.

Del paced the room. "It ain't easy running a business. You know, they say two-thirds of all businesses fail, you know that, don't you? You haven't been working in a long time. We've been in desperate straits, but I've been doing everything to keep things together for us. This hospital stuff is killing us. It's absolutely killing us. We can't afford it. And oh, that brother of yours, he had to drag us all out here to St. Augustine. That cost two arms and a leg, I'm telling you. Big, fancy hospital. Costing what it does and they still can't figure out what's wrong with you.

"I'm here all day and night with you, the boys are off somewhere else. We can't afford this, no, no, no. Look what it's doing to our finances. Sure, we owe money. We owe lots of it. I tried to keep it from you 'cause I love you and I don't want you to worry. But then that Rusty, oh, he's gotta be some kinda hero. He's no hero. He never liked me from the start. He never liked me. None of your family ever liked me. Maybe they thought that first husband of yours was a saint, I don't know. Bet he wasn't no saint a' tall. I know men. All men are the same deep down. Me, I'm a man of God. What was he, some grease monkey? Some laborer? You tellin' me they preferred him to *me*? Him to me? That's a load of hooey, a bunch of ignorant, backwoods hooey."

Del rambled on and on but Connie Jo only felt stung by a stray phrase here and there, not the bulk of it. Talking down Rusty; talking down Ben. He never even had met Ben or known Ben. What would he know about a good man like Ben Filer?

She waited him out, never interrupting, never reacting, continuously staring at the blank, hospital wall until finally Del ran out of steam—or else was simply revving up for his next lap around the track.

"Rusty's bringing a lawyer here so I can change my will."

She'd stopped him dead in his tracks again. "What?"

"You heard me," she replied in that same calm, clear monotone she'd delivered to the wall. "If everything's as you say it is, it won't matter none. My money belongs to my boys. If anything happens to me, they get it all, just like I always wanted it to be. I should probably look into my insurance money and my CDs as well, get it all back into my name, get everything back to the way it was before I met you. Anything you earned you can keep, I don't want any of it. But everything of mine goes to my boys, period."

Del expanded to fill the room. "You owe money, woman! You have debts and bills. Your name is on things. You have responsibilities. You can't go escaping responsibility by cutting me out! I'll sue, I swear I will. I'll get a lawyer, too."

"Do what you must. I'll do what I must. Far as the bills are concerned, you took that all away from me, remember? Besides, that's got nothing to do with it. Rusty will be my executor and he'll manage my finances. I'm just making sure my boys don't have any impediments between them and what's theirs."

Del quieted for a moment and Connie wondered what he was up to. She half expected he was going to be standing over her with a pillow, looking to smother her. The silence lasted so long, she was tempted to turn and look. Oh, how she did not want to do that. Where was Rusty? What was taking him so long? She thought he'd be right back.

Finally, she did turn Del's way. He was no longer facing her, but was looking out the window, his back to her. "You just had to mess things up, didn't you? You and your changing your will and all. You had to go mess things up."

# Chapter Thirty

Connie Jo Mobley's cries could be heard halfway down the hallway of the hospital. They were guttural, wordless—the sounds of an animal being killed, not a human who could speak language and communicate. Rusty, a nurse and a doctor all raced into the room together only to find Del Mobley standing rather calmly across the room, holding a large cup from the local Dairy Queen.

"I'm on fire, I'm on fire," was all anyone could make out from the screams and noises Connie Jo was making. She projectile vomited across her self, sweat pouring out of her as if she were in a sauna. "I can't feel nothin'! It's creeping up on me. It's creeping up!"

The doctor hit a button and more help arrived. Soon, Connie Jo's bed was being wheeled down the hallway at a racer's pace, nurses and doctors pushing and chasing after it. Rusty jogged after her for a few paces, then instead turned and went back into the room. There stood Del Mobley, holding the large cup as if he were an innocent child without a care in the world, the straw daintily pinched between two of his fingers, stirring mindlessly.

Rusty looked at him, then took a quick glance around the room itself. His eyes came to rest upon the emergency button next to the bed. "Why didn't you call for help? Why?"

Rusty got all red in the face and began making his way over towards Del, but Del did something unexpected. Instead of bracing himself for a fight or moving towards Rusty in order to engage with him, he made a beeline to the sink, quickly pouring away what was left in the cup. It took Rusty off guard to say the least, and he looked on as the brown, milky substance swirled down the drain. As he watched, Del not only emptied the cup, but he also washed it out and rinsed it in steamy, hot water as if he were trying to sterilize it or something. It was a totally incongruous act, given what was going on around him—his wife on a gurney, headed for the operating room, his brother-in-law looming over him, accusing him of not caring.

Finally, Rusty slapped the cup, wet with water, out of Del's hands. "What is the matter with you? What did you do to my sister?"

Del Mobley looked at Rusty in an infantile manner, sincerely perplexed. "I bought her a milkshake. She likes them."

Rusty Roberts' face scowled and reddened. "Why aren't you with her?"

Del remained nonplussed. "Why aren't you?"

This was getting nowhere. Rusty turned and ran back down the hall in the direction they were taking his sister while Del remained behind. Rusty's mind was torn between issues—was Connie going to die? What had happened to her? What was up with Del? Why was he so placid? Had he done something to her? If so, what?

By the time Rusty got to where they were working on Connie Jo, a nurse gently but firmly stopped him from entering the room. "She's seizing. They're working on her."

"Seizing?"

"Her heart. She's having seizures. They're trying to get her stabilized."

Rusty went all flushed, his jaw slack. "How? Why?" But no answers were forthcoming.

A few minutes later, his wife, Colby, came to where he was, and he filled her in on what was going on. A doctor who had been in with Connie Jo came out to give an update. "Your sister had seven cardiac seizures in forty-five minutes. We're going to install a pacemaker to try to stabilize her, but it's very iffy right now. You may want to call the rest of your family. This is bad. I don't want to sugarcoat it for you, but it's bad."

Colby buried her head in Rusty's chest, and Rusty consoled her despite how upset he was as well. "Doc, do they have any idea what caused it?"

The doctor shook his head slightly. "We're not completely sure. We've been guessing at quite a few things, but she keeps responding erratically. Some of the things we thought it could be, she wouldn't be getting relapses right here under our noses."

"Things like what?" Rusty asked, hoping to understand.

The doctor glanced at the ceiling for a second. "Poisoning…"

"Poisoning?"

"But like I said, that wouldn't explain how she could get better, then worse, then better again lying right here in the hospital."

Rusty wanted to pull the doctor closer to him, to make him stay and discuss the case, but when Rusty went mute for a moment the doctor took that opportunity to head back into the operating room, leaving Rusty and Colby behind.

Time went on. Connie's younger brother, Kirby, arrived, bringing with him their mother and father, as did her sisters, Kelly Sue and Florence, bringing B.J. and Gabriel with them. They huddled together in a small waiting room outside where the doctors were working frantically on Connie Jo. All were there…except for Del Mobley, who presumably was still back in her hospital room, all by his lonesome without a care in the world.

The same doctor came out from time to time, giving them updates, but the hours dragged on and Connie Jo was still not out of the woods yet. Once, when the doctor came out, Rusty put his arm around his shoulder and pulled him aside, away from the others.

"Can we talk a minute, Doc?" he asked softly. The man followed him into a far off corner. "Doc, you say you're investigating poisoning?"

"Yes. Most everything else comes up negative. But again, poisoning wouldn't explain why she's having such distress now. Here in the hospital, we control her diet and we've made sure that nothing she's taken in could possibly cause a reaction like this."

Rusty didn't know how to say what he knew had to come next. He wiped his mouth and finally whispered, "I can't rightly prove it, but I have reason to believe…*strong* reason to believe…that her husband might be trying to kill her."

He paused, dreading the reaction he'd get. Surely, by accusing another man, a minister no less, he'd either be considered crazy or a prime suspect himself. Oh, how he had led a life of never bearing false witness against another. But the evidence was piling and piling up around him and Rusty Roberts had no idea what else to do.

Instead of jerking away from him, the doctor calmly looked Rusty in the face and said, "I'll be right back."

*Oh, this is not good, not good at all,* Rusty thought. A moment passed and a nurse—a somewhat older woman—joined the doctor as they walked back to the corner where Rusty was still standing.

"Reverent Roberts, this is Hannah Socker. She's the head nurse on your sister's floor. What you were saying before—do you honestly believe something is going on with your brother-in-law and Mrs. Mobley?"

Rusty looked at the doctor and the nurse. *This is the most trying time of my life,* he thought. But he tried to calm himself and say a silent prayer to the Lord, asking not merely for strength but for guidance as well.

"Yes, yes I do. We've suspected for a long time that he's been hitting her, as well as her kids. Earlier today, I went to their house. I picked up their mail. They had a letter from the IRS. They owe a lot of money, a lot. And while I was there, the house blew up."

The shock made both the doctor and the nurse back up a step.

"No, I'm not kidding you. I went in, smelled gas, and then I barely got out before the place blew to smithereens. Her son and I could have been killed. You can call the fire marshal in Gainesville, he'll tell you all about it.

"The thing is, she had money when she came into this marriage and he had none. She's a widow. Her husband died young and left her a nice bit of money, but now it's all gone and there's all this money they owe—*he* owes. He doesn't work anymore and he could never hold a job before, either. He put his name all over everything she has and he never shows her the bills. I know she doesn't spend wastefully. It's got to all be him."

Rusty was getting himself all worked up and he was afraid he was going far off topic. He collected himself and tried to wrap it all up. "I believe he only wants her for her money. I also know he's been giving her food and things since she's been here in the hospital. When she just took a turn today, I found him in her room dumping a milkshake down the drain and rinsing the cup."

The doctor and nurse looked at one another, then back at Rusty. "Reverend Roberts, we're going to call the sheriff's department. Will you be sticking around?"

"Yes, yes of course I will," he replied.

"Good. We want you to tell them what you just told us."

# Chapter Thirty-One

Connie Jo Mobley lay in her hospital bed back in her room, surrounded by her parents, her siblings, her children and her husband. The tableau was like a wake, for Connie Jo was unconscious and completely unaware of her surroundings. Tubes fed into her everywhere, and it seemed as if nothing but machines were keeping her alive. A nurse and a doctor stood by her side.

"I'm glad y'all could make it," the doctor began. "I've always believe in being as honest with people as possible. Connie Jo has undergone a tremendous trauma and the next twenty-four hours will be crucial. If she makes it through the night, it will be a miracle. She may pull through, but it will be touch and go."

Kelly Sue was perhaps the most distraught, feeling the

unique twinges of pain only a twin could experience. "Doctor, is there anything we can do?" she said through tears.

"Pray. Just pray. Y'all can stay, but please, she's very fragile. If any of you have a cold or anything at all, try not to touch her. Wash your hands and don't breathe on her if you can manage it. We don't need anyone introducing any germs into her environment. But that's about all. She's in God's hands now."

The Roberts family formed a cordon around their downed daughter. Del Mobley stood off to the side, more likely than not because he simply could not break on through and get any closer. No one spoke to him, which caused a look of confused frustration on his face. This was a man used to being the center of attention in any room he occupied, but not now, not today. Instead, it seemed as if everyone else there wanted him to be gone. Still, he said nothing, for fear, perhaps, of making his own situation worse.

A bit later, another doctor entered the room, looked over at Connie Jo and the rest, then headed straight towards Del. "Reverend Mobley, I'm going to need to take you for some tests."

Del Mobley looked confused. "You must mean my wife. She's over there. She's the sick one. I'm fine."

The young doctor persisted. "We're checking for possible home carcinogens. We'd like to test you, too, even though you're not showing any signs of trouble at the moment."

Del turned his head from side to side, obviously

uncomfortable and unhappy, looking somewhere for help but not getting any from Connie Jo's people. "If it's something from the home, why don't you just go there?"

"'Cause your house blew up," snapped Rusty, looking up angrily.

Del shot Rusty an equally bitter look but began following the doctor, knowing he had little choice but to cooperate. "Just a minute," he said as he was almost out of the room. He then gently pushed apart Colby Roberts and Connie Jo's sister, Florence, bent down and said to a still-unconscious Connie Jo, "I'll be right back, darlin'. Everything's gonna be all right. I love you, you know that. I love you more than life itself."

Del dipped his head even lower and planted a kiss right on the corner of Connie Jo's lips, right next to a tube that was inserted into her mouth and down her throat.

"They told you not to kiss her or touch her!" shouted Rusty, reaching across people and grabbing Del's shirt collar. He kept that hold on him as he stumbled around, until he finally was able to get enough leverage to pull him away from the bed so that he could push Del forcefully against a wall. "They told you not to kiss her!" he spat in his face as he screamed.

Del, who was certainly every bit as large and manly as Rusty and could have pushed him away and gotten into a real donnybrook with him, instead remained placid, blinking rapidly as if attempting to produce crocodile tears where real ones did not exist. With a croak in his voice he had no trouble feigning, he said, "I forgot. I'm sorry. I love her so. She's my whole life. If anything happens to her, I'll die. I'll surely die."

As he finished his sentence, he turned towards the doctor as if to check his audience to see how he was doing. The doctor seemed unmoved, just impatient.

Rusty released his grip. Del straightened himself, raised his chin an inch or two higher, and followed the doctor out.

About two minutes went by and another doctor, along with a hospital administrator and a state policeman, entered Connie Jo's room. They turned to Rusty and said, "Okay, he's gone. Let's go." They proceeded to raise the handrails on Connie Jo's bed and release the locking mechanisms on the bed's wheels.

"What's going on?" asked Connie Jo's mother.

"Trust me, I've got this under control. These good people are here for Connie Jo," said Rusty as he assisted by gently nudging everyone away from the now-moving bed.

The bed rolled briskly down the hall, through a set of double doors, and made a number of twists and turns before entering another room. It was not a surgical suite nor a treatment room of any sort, just another hospital room like the one out of which she had just been wheeled. From time to time, as they trailed the moving bed, the family turned to one another and particularly to Rusty, to repeat a simple question: "What's going on?" But no one who knew gave any answers.

"Whatcha want? Blood?" said Del Mobley as he began rolling up his sleeve.

A stern-faced nurse replied, "No. Urine sample. Go in there," she said as she pointed towards a bathroom.

"Now?" Del asked. The nurse looked at him as if he had asked as stupid a question as he indeed had. "Of course now. I ain't got all day," she said as she handed him a plastic cup.

Del stared at it like he had never seen one before. "Uh… actually, I just went. What'll I do?"

The nurse was getting more and more perturbed. "Take a drink. Fountain's out in the hallway. Make it snappy."

Del's face went through a variety of emotions, at least one of them being anger, as if he wanted to snap right back at this insolent woman in green hospital scrubs. Instead, though, he held back his temper, paused, and then said, "I have a soda I left in my car out in the parking lot. I'll go there and bring it in. That should do the trick."

He turned and literally ran out the door lest the nurse try to stop him. A few minutes later he returned, no soda in his hand. "I finished it. You say the bathroom's in here?" he asked, smiling.

"Yeah. I didn't need a gallon or nothing. You could've used the water fountain in the hall."

But Del Mobley didn't bother to argue since he already had won his point. A minute later he came back and proudly handed a near-full cup to the nurse, who took it from him in her rubber-gloved hand; he stood before her as if he half expected a compliment on his ability to release water. She turned away from him, lay it on a metal table, picked up a pair of scissors and said, "Now I need some hair."

"Wuh?"

"Hair, I need some hair," she said as she came towards him with the surgical scissors. "Sit," she added as she kicked a short stool on wheels so that it appeared right behind him. Dutifully, he bent his knees and sat.

"I don't want you messing up my hair…" he began, but she quickly cut him off.

"I usually just take from the back of the neck. You won't miss it a bit," she said as she snipped before he could protest any more.

"Ouch!"

"Sorry, but it helps if I get some root. You're not bleeding or anything, no need to worry."

Still, Del reached around behind his head to feel if everything that needed to be there still was.

The nurse was behind him again, this time running a curtain around a ceiling track until it surrounded them. "Drop your pants."

"What?"

"I need some more hair," she replied while she wielded the scissors in an even more disconcerting way.

"I don't get it," Del stammered.

"Pubic hair. Drop your trousers, please. I'm a nurse. Ain't nothing down there I haven't seen before."

"But, but—"

"Reverend, I'm doing this for your own good. You may have been exposed to something. Please, drop your pants. If you want, I'll ask a male attending to step in if it'll make you feel more comfortable."

Del stared at her for a long time, as if he were waiting for her to admit it was all a joke, but the nurse's serious expression never changed. "Usually I have to buy a woman a drink before we get to this point," he joked, but he regretted it the moment he'd said it as her scissors aimed right towards his manhood.

After she cut, she kept her scissors at the ready. "Hands."

"What about 'em?"

"I need fingernails. If they're too short, I can do toenails, too. It don't matter at all to me."

"I've never been through such a thing. This is crazy stuff," Del replied, but the nurse's demanding demeanor caused an almost-automatic response—Del holding out his hands, palms to the floor, as she cut away. "This manicure gonna cost me anything?" he said, again trying to add levity to the proceedings.

"Oh, it might cost you plenty."

Connie Jo Mobley slowly began to regain consciousness. All around her she saw the faces of the people she loved and who loved her right back. Everyone, it seemed, but Del Mobley, her husband. Groggily, she tried to speak; the tube that had been down her throat was now blissfully removed, but her throat was still excruciatingly sore. She looked around, dazed and slightly confused.

"You're in another room, sis," said Rusty as he moved up towards her head. But Connie Jo didn't question that, nor did she question anything. Instead, she just looked from face to face to face.

"I died," she finally said softly. "I know I died. I was in a battle, but every time I wanted to surrender I saw my boys and I kept on fighting."

B.J. and Gabe moved up towards their mother's open arms and she cradled them lovingly. "I...I didn't want them to spend the rest of their lives without me. I didn't want them to be left with…" And her voice trailed off.

"Are you looking for Del?" Rusty said calmly yet authoritatively.

Tears welled up in Connie Jo's eyes.

"He's not here," said Rusty. "Did you want him here? We thought we could talk a while without him here. Are you comfortable with that?"

Connie Jo looked around some more, trying to clear her head. "Fine," she replied.

From behind her beloved family strode forward a state policeman. "Mrs. Mobley, I'm Officer Bradbury. The doctors think they know what happened to you insofar as your condition. Ma'am, you've been poisoned with arsenic."

"How'd that happen?" Connie Jo replied weakly.

"We believe it was intentionally induced. Ma'am, I need you to make a statement and I'd like you to be as truthful as possible. Were you and your husband having marital problems?" He paused and looked at Connie Jo, who in turn twisted her head from side to side, looking at B.J. and Gabe, looking at her parents, looking at Rusty, Kirby and her sisters and sisters-in-law. "Ma'am, did he hit you or your children? Did he hit any of you in anger?"

Connie Jo paused pensively, then finally gave herself up to God. "Yes, God, yes he did. I'm sorry."

"Why are you sorry? You have nothing to feel sorry about. He hit you—did you hit *him*?" interjected Rusty.

"No, I never hit him. I never meant him any harm. All I ever wanted to do was love him and support him. He said he loved me. He's a man of God. I was a preacher's wife." But by now Connie Jo was all but unintelligible, blubbering uncontrollably. Kelly Sue reached over to hug and console her.

"Connie Jo," said Rusty, "we've drawn up this restraining order. They'll be bringing charges against Del, but in the meantime, we want you to be safe and away from the man."

Connie Jo seemed acquiescent, but then a little confused. "Why?"

The state trooper spoke again. "Ma'am, they tested your husband for arsenic to see if it was environmental. There was an incredibly high concentration in his urine, but none at all in his hair or nails. To properly test for arsenic poisoning, you need urine, hair, fingernails and also pubic hair. The hospital tested you and the numbers were off the charts. Ma'am, we think your husband poisoned you. We think he's been poisoning you for a long time now. We think he's even been poisoning you right here in the hospital. We think he dumped some in his own urine just to throw us off, but he didn't know we'd be testing his hair and nails as well. No other part of his body turned up any of it. That, the hitting, the abuse, the money problems, the two suspicious insurance claims on your homes—we think your husband was trying to kill you, probably for money."

Connie Jo's eyes widened. She was no longer lethargic but was awakened fully by adrenaline.

"Connie Jo, we've had them draw up a criminal complaint, a restraining order against Del, and we have a lawyer here who has redrawn your will and has drafted a petition to the court for you to take Del's name off of documents for assets that were clearly yours prior to your marriage to him. We've even drafted documents contesting his adoption of the boys. We're claiming fraud and intent to defraud. The lawyer's even ready to begin legal separation and divorce proceedings for you. All you have to do is sign," said Rusty.

Connie Jo, while now wide awake, remained in a state of shock. "Honey, I know it's a lot to take in, but we're here for you, we're all here for you. We're your family. The man tried to kill you. But he's been stopped. We're all here to help you put this behind you," said her mother. "Connie Jo, dear, it's time to come home."

Connie Jo breathed steadily, hyperaware of each and every breath she took. She continued to scan the room. Faces. Nothing but faces. All of the faces, she knew, were filled with love and concern for her. Next to them stood the serious-yet-determined faces of policemen, nurses and doctors. Each face seemed to be in agreement.

Kelly Sue handed her twin sister a pen and swung over a tray stand. "Momma's right. We are the people who love you. Even the doctors and the nurses, Connie Jo, they love you, too. You've been through a nightmare, I know. But now you're awake. Sign the papers and the nightmare will be over."

Connie Jo kept looking from face to face. She was like Dorothy at the end of *The Wizard of Oz*. Yes, these were the people who loved her. Del would have tried to tell her they were all wrong and only he was right, but the more she looked into all those faces, even the faces of B.J. and Gabe, the more she knew these were the ones who were right. Del Mobley was wrong. Del Mobley was wrong.

# Chapter Thirty-Two

It was as if the lone figure in the front pew of the church had somehow found the only quiet spot amidst a loud and raucous party. She sat alone, facing front towards the altar, no one else in any other seat of the large, high-ceilinged church.

"Hey! Whatchu doin' there? Everyone's waiting for the mother of the groom. They want to take pictures and head on out for the reception." The booming voice belonged to Reverend Rusty Roberts.

Still, the figure, which looked like nothing more than a blond head atop the back of the pew, did not move. Rusty briskly approached, but when he finally got to the front of the church he slowed his pace and carefully studied the person there, sitting all alone by choice. "Connie Jo. Connie

Jo. C'mon, they've waiting," he said more softly now, more slowly now.

Connie Jo Filer—who had dropped her last name from her second marriage, as had her two children, who were now known again as B.J. and Gabriel Filer—did not meet her brother's eyes. "I don't belong here," she whispered, dropping her head in shame.

"No, you belong out with all the other people. It's time…"

But Rusty's voice trailed off as he realized she meant something far deeper than he had first imagined. Slowly, he slid in next to her. Since she did not raise her head to meet his gaze, he, too, stared at the altar, focusing on the large, wooden cross at its center.

Finally, she spoke once more. "Do you know I haven't been to church in years?"

"Yep," he replied without judgment.

"Haven't felt like it. Felt I would be a hypocrite if I did. I have all these terrible, terrible thoughts and feelings deep down inside of me."

"Wanna talk about it?"

Connie Jo shook her head ever so slightly. "Now's not the best time. B.J., Jolene, Gabe and Tanya will be waiting. This is their day—big, double wedding. I don't want to ruin it."

"So you'll put on a brave face and pretend everything is alright, right?"

"That's kind of rude of you, if I must say so," she replied.

"I can get ruder," Rusty responded. "I could say that you've been wearing a false face for years now and I think if you really wanted to give your sons and their new brides a wedding present maybe it would be that you'd open up and talk about why you're sitting here all by your lonesome. I have time. I'll stay with you."

Connie Jo let out a long huff and batted her eyes, which were wet from all sorts of mixed emotions. "If you'd have told me eleven years ago I'd be alive and sitting here on my sons' wedding day, I'd have told you you were crazy. I was dead. Dead to rights. They say eight hundred units of arsenic will kill you. I had ten thousand, four hundred eighty-one. Can you believe it? That's death more than a dozen times over."

"It's a miracle alright," Rusty said, stretching back in his seat, rolling his arm around his sister's shoulder. "Couldn't possibly tell you where miracles come from, now could I?" he tweaked.

"Real funny, preacher man." But Connie Jo found no humor in it at all.

"You gonna tell me directly why it is you gave up on the church, or do I have to drag it out of you?"

"I tried going once or twice," she said. "But then I'd look at the man in the pulpit and wonder, *How do I know he's not a phony and a hypocrite, too?*"

"Yeah, you got burned pretty darn good," Rusty answered, surprising her with his candor.

"I mean, I married the devil himself. How could that man…" And she paused for a moment as anger seethed out of her, because for over the past eleven years she had not been able to so much as mention the name Del Mobley. "How could he preach fire and brimstone when he was not a true man of God, when he was a thief, a liar, a murderer?" And her tears began to flow.

Rusty took his sister's head against his shoulder and comforted her. "Ain't quite murder. You're still alive. And they never really proved he killed his father, either, though you and I both know it's highly likely he did. I guess compared to his old man, you're just a victim of bum luck, right?"

"Why're you bein' so cold, Rusty? Can't you see I'm upset?"

"I'm just letting you get it all out of your system, see what kind of crazy words you're gonna come up with to justify the way you feel. Maybe if you talk long enough, you'll hear your own nonsense and I won't have to say a thing."

"Rusty, what's your point?"

Rusty let out a sigh. "Sis, it goes like this. Let's take Brother Del—"

"Don't you call him that. Don't you ever say his name and attach some sort of honor to it."

"But he *was* a preacher. That's why you say you can't sit in the house of the Lord no more. So let's deal with it. You say he preached the gospel. You're right. Now, try to take your personal animosity out of it for a moment and lemme ask you, did he do it well? Were his sermons blasphemous?

Did he change the word of God? Twist it? Make stuff up that wasn't there in the big book?"

Connie Jo was angry and tightlipped. "The sermons were fine."

"Yep, that ol' boy could give a heck of a sermon when he wanted to. Snakes can use the word of God as well as the righteous man."

"His tongue shoulda fallen out of his head. His mouth shoulda filled with hot ashes."

"Yeah, that's a vengeful, Old-Testament God you're talkin' about right there, yes siree," Rusty replied.

Connie Jo turned her head to face her brother. "Is this supposed to be helping? 'Cause I ain't feeling any better, just so's you know."

"Oh, I could make it even worse if I wanted to, sis. They went and arrested the man and then—"

"And then nothing! They caught him dead to rights. Means, motive, opportunity—all that stuff from the TV crime shows. Two grand juries. Sheriff's office givin' him that polygraph test that he failed miserably—"

"Couldn't use that in a court of law."

"I know, Rusty, but still."

"Did I ever tell you this one?" Rusty asked. "During the first grand jury, I went out to a Shoney's for lunch. Know who I found there? Brother Del. I thank the Lord every night He gave me the strength not to kill the man where he stood, I swear."

"I went up to him, though. I went up to him and he stood there, big as day, almost darin' me to pop him one or pull out a gun or something. We was outside and there were people all around, so he knew what he was doin'. He had witnesses if he needed them.

"I don't know what I said. It don't matter none, 'cause all I knew was the rage I felt deep down inside. I coulda been speaking in tongues for all I know. But he got the gist of it, as did everybody else in that there parking lot.

"Once I finished my diatribe, he smiled that obnoxious smirk of his and pointed up at the traffic light right across from us. He said, 'You see that light right there? Well, if you don't see me run it, how you gonna prove I ever did?' Man, that got my goat. He knew what he done. He knew it, the police knew it, the grand jury knew it—"

"Yeah, everybody knew it but that prosecutor lady," Connie Jo interrupted. "Woman had more pride than guts or brains. Kept saying how she was 'undefeated.' Undefeated. Thought she was running the Dallas Cowboys instead of a prosecutor's office. She kept stalling and stalling, saying she wanted more evidence, more evidence. What more could she have gotten? What more could she have needed? She had everything 'cept a videotape of Del actually doing it to me!"

Rusty scooted down a little lower in his seat, relaxing, strangely enough. "Yeah, I'd say it was about as frustrating a thing as a person could ever have happen to them." He paused for effect.

"You makin' fun of my pain?" Connie Jo asked.

"I've never been so sincere in my life. Man literally got away with murder. He ruined you. He darn near killed you, beat on you, beat up your boys, stole their real father's name from them and stole all your money. What more evil could one person bring upon another in this here world of ours? And all you did was open up your heart and your home to him, 'cause he was supposed to be a man of God."

"Rusty, that's what I've been sayin' here! So what are we here talkin' about?"

Rusty calmly let it all wash over her to see if she understood at all where he was going. "You feel betrayed."

"Right! I feel very betrayed."

"Betrayed by Del Mobley."

"Betrayed by Del Mobley," she repeated.

"Betrayed by God."

Connie Jo stiffened as if she'd just been hit.

"Betrayed by God, right? That's why you haven't been going to church. God betrayed you, right? That's what I hear you sayin'."

"No…Yes…No," Connie Jo said, confused and muted in her tone.

Rusty took his time and then answered, "Imagine how betrayed Jesus felt. Now there's a man who got betrayed. He was betrayed something awful. Can you imagine the crisis of faith He suffered through? And He didn't *nearly* die—He died, period, and then on the third day he rose again to sit at the right hand of God the father."

Connie Jo started getting agitated. "But...But I'm not comparing myself to Jesus. That's blasphemous."

"I never said you were, and I wouldn't suggest you do."

"But...Listen, I know others have suffered more than I have. I'm not sitting here saying 'boo hoo' and 'nobody knows the trouble I've seen.' People suffer and die each day, I know that. But I was betrayed by a *man of God,* don't you understand that? That man was the kind of man I was supposed to be able to put my faith and trust in. He stood up there and he preached the word of God," she said as she pointed to the vacant pulpit.

"And we already said that the words he spoke when he was up there were true."

"And that is why I am in this predicament! We've been goin' around and around and here we are, right back where we started," said Connie Jo angrily.

"Connie Jo." Rusty leaned forward to look at his sister. "You're pointing at the pulpit and you're imagining a man standing there, a flesh-and-blood man. But whoever stands there is simply a vessel of God. The moment that man, any man, takes that spot and misrepresents God's word, everyone within earshot will rise up and carry him off as a blasphemer.

"Del Mobley was a lot of things, most all of them bad and evil, but when he stood on that altar he did not misspeak the word of the Lord. He inspired people and touched their souls. I know, it pains me as much to say that as it must pain you to hear it. And because that man was so evil, imagine the miracle of God's strength that He still used Del as a vessel for His word. What I'm trying to say is, we come here to God's house not for the man who stands before us to spread God's word, but for God's word itself.

"There is an ego to this job of mine. I know it, and maybe Del Mobley knew it on some level, but he could not control it. You get up in front of a congregation and you're praising God's name and pretty soon you're getting all that love sent right back to you. If you don't truly understand the love of the Lord, you begin, like Del did, to believe you are something special, something more special than all those people sitting in the pews. You feel the love they have for Jesus and you start to be seduced by it. In Del's case, you start to become sort of messiah yourself, which is as blasphemous a thing as ever there was.

"What Del said when he was preaching was never the problem. It was that he didn't humble himself before the Lord. He wanted the congregation to humble themselves before *him*, and that's wrong, that's a sin. He also demanded that his woman and his family do the same towards him at home, and that was where he made your life so miserable. That was what he did to other women, too, you know that. And that child of his, Rae. That was what made her life so hard and so full of confusion and hate. Did you ever pray for her?"

It was the last question Connie Jo could have imagined. "Pray for her? I hardly even knew the girl. I only saw her once, that one time she came to my house right before Del and I got married."

"When he died…" Rusty paused for a moment. "I never

told you this. I know you were torn about the whole thing. You said some terrible things about Del when you found out and so did I."

"They said it was painful and I was glad to hear it. I only wished that cancer had stayed with him even longer so the pain would have gone on and on until he realized the terrible things he had done in his lifetime," added Connie Jo.

"I know, I know," said Rusty, "but I was there for you. I heard you out and I let you vent on and on about him when you heard about it. I figured if I got you to spew it all out at once, you wouldn't keep doing it and poisoning those two fine boys of yours by goin' on and on about it every day for years thereafter.

"But here's the part I kept from you. I went and looked up that Rae gal. I found her and I found Vivian, his first wife. Talkin' to them, I even found that woman he took up with between Vivian and you. And then I found that other woman with all the money who he took up with after you left him. Every one of them hated that man so. I must admit, I found myself getting caught up in it. I'm just a man, too, you know?

"And I don't even rightly know why I even did it all in the first place. I don't know, maybe I was searching my own soul. Or maybe, at times, I was just looking to vent like I encouraged you to. When I was with you, you talked and I listened. Maybe, I thought, with these other women, I would listen and then I would add your story to theirs and we could all get angry together, I don't know. Kinda get it out of my own system before it poisoned me, too. So there were high and low motivations going on all around me.

"Anyway, he left them all bitter and damaged, just like you're feeling right now. But the one I felt the most for was this Rae girl. She was so young when he got to her. She never had a chance. She's grown up hard, hard as barbed wire and bristles. These other women, they knew happiness in their lives and times without the kind of bitterness he left them with. Some eventually got over the man. Vivian, she's pretty much moved on now that Rae's all grown up. The woman in between, she seems to have gotten over him, mostly. She was his secret woman—they never really lived together as man and wife. The last one is still dealing with it.

"But Rae, God, I pray every night for that Rae. She never felt security, she never felt love, and now she's encapsulated herself in a hard shell and I don't know if she'll ever come out of it. I pray for that girl. I pray for her soul."

Connie Jo sat in silence for a time. "When I met her, she seemed like a hard gal to feel sorry for, but then again maybe not. I can see how he could have made her that way. Or maybe there's a lot of him inside of her. He was just so evil. But Rusty, that's not the part that's so hard to get over. I've had to get over Ben's death and there ain't a day I don't think about him in some way or another. But that's been a gentler and sweeter pain."

"You know Ben's with God," said Rusty.

"Yes…" But her voice trailed off again. "I have trouble saying things like that now. It used to come so naturally.

This, this here, sitting in church, this was always the easiest, most-natural thing in the world for me. Now I feel Del's taken that away. Del Mobley's taken God away from my life." And she openly wept.

Rusty patted her on the shoulder, something that almost startled her. In some dark crevice of her mind, she almost wanted or expected him to castigate her or maybe even slap her. Del would have slapped her. Del had slapped her at almost any provocation, but often it was when they clashed about the Lord. He slapped her when she claimed he was sinning against God and against man. He also slapped her when she was at her wit's end and openly moaned to God about how unhappy she was with her life—the life that Del Mobley had created around her.

But Rusty Roberts wasn't like that. When they were kids, they'd roughhoused around like any other tykes, but that had been a long, long time ago. Now Rusty was all purity and gentility—the sort of thing she realized she was looking for in a man, in Del Mobley. Oh, how disappointed she was that she had selected so blindly and so wrongly in settling in with Del.

"Have you tried talking to anybody 'bout this?"

"Other than you?" she asked.

Rusty had thought maybe he hadn't been getting through to his sister because they had so much history together.

"No, no, not really. Vardemen Shirey came to visit me a few times and maybe we got into it—*he* got into it. But I just have a hard time being ministered to now."

"Vardemen's a good man. Good man," Rusty said wistfully.

"He set me up with the devil," Connie Jo replied.

"Naw, Vardemen didn't know 'bout that. Frankly, he and I've been talking over the years. I don't think a day goes by he doesn't ask the Lord's forgiveness for not intervening sooner or deeper, 'specially when he found out 'bout the poisoning. You'd-a thought he was going to turn himself in to the police as an accessory. The man was torn to pieces. A lot of people felt that way. *I* felt that way."

"You, Rusty? You didn't do nothing wrong. You didn't like him from the start. You always acted like you saw a snake in the grass when you looked at him and you tried every which way you could to warn me off, but I wasn't having none of it."

"Did I make you mad?"

Connie Jo thought. "I could never be mad at you, Rusty. I got the best family in the world." And she hugged him for emphasis.

"Yeah, that's quite a blessing. You've been truly blessed, Connie Jo Filer."

Connie Jo looked up at him. "You still nagging on me 'bout something?"

"Well, let's do an inventory. You grew up right, met and married a fine man—"

"Did not!"

"I meant the first one. Had two fine young boys—"

"And then Ben died."

"And then Ben went to his maker. It was tragic, but God only gives us what we can handle and you handled it."

"Did not."

"Did, too. You were as good a single mother as could be. And then God sent you the sort of man you'd been praying for, but he turned out to be a test of your faith, a test you're still not through taking."

Connie Jo pulled away again. "Tested…What did I do so wrong that I needed to be tested so? He tried to kill me. Kill me!"

"And you lived. What did you say? Eight hundred units could kill you and you had ten thousand somethin'? What do you call that?"

"A miracle," Connie Jo said disgustedly, under her breath.

"And where do miracles come from?"

Connie Jo simply hung her head.

Rusty moved closer to her again. "Just as God brought Del Mobley into your life, He also performed a miracle by letting you live. You said it yourself—you should by all means be dead, dead to rights. I mean, this one wasn't even close. Twelve, thirteen times over, whatever, I ain't no mathematician, but medical science can't explain such a thing. You received a miracle, and what have you done with it? What have you done, Connie Jo?"

Connie Jo's eyes got wet again, yet she balled up her fists as if ready to strike. "I raised two boys to men all by myself. I did it after they'd been so traumatized I could hardly even recognize them. B.J.'d been cowed into having no self-confidence at all. He used to be such a happy boy, but he spent years just withdrawing, being quiet, retreating into his own little world, afraid of everything and everybody. I couldn't believe when he brought Jolene home the first time. I'd begun to think he'd never get up the nerve to go out and meet a girl. Del Mobley took his childhood away from him, scarred him.

"And Gabe, well, Gabe couldn't even believe what happened. He tried to blame me at times. Del had him so snookered, giving him preferential treatment and all. That was his game—to try to split us all apart, turn us against one another."

"But he came around," said Rusty.

"By the grace of—" And she cut herself off.

"Yep, by the grace of God—again. God's grace gave you another miracle. That's at least two, but there are so many more, one cannot even count. Connie Jo," he said as he turned to face her, his hands on either side of her, holding on to her shoulders, "I've had a good life, a simple life. Probably the biggest drama I ever had was the day I almost got blown up going to your house to get you your clothes when you were in the hospital. That was *my* miracle, 'cause one minute more and I'd-a been killed.

"But Connie Jo, God granted you all these trials and all these miracles for a reason. You've got to believe that H chose you and I don't know why, but you'v
follow Him and give yourself back up to H

this is not my house. I only get to preach in it. This is God's house. Whenever you see a place like this, know that—know that Del Mobley was wrong. He'd always say 'my church,' or 'I gotta get me my own church.' A church don't belong to anybody but God. We come here to be inspired and to inspire others, nothing more. You, Connie Jo, you are a living, breathing inspiration if you choose to be."

"Rusty, you telling me I should start preaching?"

"If you want to."

Connie Jo shook her head with embarrassment. "Rusty, that's not my style. I'm a quiet gal. I could never go up there in the pulpit and do the things that you do."

"Connie Jo, there's more than one kind of ministering. I do what I do 'cause it suits me. Other people in the choir, they've got singing voices I could only dream of having and that's their personal ministry to the Lord.

"Connie Jo, you need to first embrace why it is you're here on God's Earth. You are a miracle of God's love. God loves you and that's why he's brought you here this day, alive and well. By bringing the boys 'round, by helping B.J. and Gabriel get to this very special day, standing before the congregation and the eyes of the Lord in holy marriage, you've been ministering to them all this time—"

"Rusty, that's just a mother's job, nothing else."

"And that's my point. You've proved you could do this. But even B.J. and Gabe, they know all about your love, your mother's love for them, but they've probably forgotten where that comes from and what truly inspires it. *You've* forgotten where it comes from and what inspires it. You've received a miracle and you haven't come to terms with where it came from and what responsibility goes along with it.

"Connie Jo, God saved you. God saved your life. Do you get it? Do you understand that?" he said as he gripped her shoulders even more firmly, almost shaking her with his passion.

Connie Jo's eyes spilled over with tears. "Yes. Yes, I've been a bad woman,"

"No, no you haven't. Don't say that." And he hugged her, her face wet against his shirt. "You just forgot some things, that's all. But you can come back. You can come back."

"Oh, Rusty, what should I do?"

Rusty guided her away so he could look her in the eye. "Why are you alive today?"

"God!"

"That's right. Connie Jo, square yourself with God. Praise His name and know in your heart of hearts what He has done for you. Know that this miracle was given to you for a reason, and live out that reason the rest of your days. Tell your boys. Tell B.J. and Gabe. Tell them why you are here and ask them to pray with you and thank God with you. And then, then I want you to go to all the people who have entered your life since Del Mobley came around. Many of them have lost faith, too. They need solace, and some of them need guidance. Pray for them, pray for them all.

"Think of all those people in the congregations Del preached to. Many of those people are as confused as you are, wandering around life, thinking they've been betrayed by God and Jesus. Pray for them. Find them and comfort them. You can't believe the impact you could have on those people's lives, Connie Jo. Seeing you, hearing you, hearing your story and about your crisis of faith and how you came around to realize that God has a plan for us all—that could bring them back to God.

"Vardemen. He's such a good man. He still preaches the gospel, but he's been a tormented soul since Del came into your life. Pray for him. Go to him. Give him peace. Let him know your soul's been restored and you forgive him as God forgives him. Inspire him to go out with renewed vigor to the people who listen to him.

"Exa. I know, Exa's been quite defensive at times. That's the way folks can be when things like this happen. Her way of getting through each day is to try to absolve herself of any responsibility for supporting and believing in Del and choosing him instead of you at times. Go to her. Pray for her. You'll find that what she's been doing is simply holding herself together, but she's been in pain, too, just handling it in another way. I know that deep down she loves you. She wants your forgiveness, even if she's never asked for it. Humble yourself before her and she will humble herself before you."

Connie Jo wept so hard, she shook. "I'm sorry. I'm so, so sorry I ever lost my way."

"Shh, shhh," Rusty said. "I never said you lost your way. I'm not the one to say such a thing. I can't judge you. I'm not worthy of judging you. Only God can judge any of us. This here thing, this is between you and God. I'm just here to try to help you work it out."

"Del, Del made me feel bad," she said through sniffles. "Any time I crossed him, he said I was being a bad Christian woman, and that's how I've felt these past 'leven years, prob'ly even longer. At times I thought that's why I got so sick."

"Connie Jo, you were never a bad woman in the eyes of the Lord, even all this time you questioned His motives and His love. Just embrace Him and embrace His word. Then go out and do good works in His name. Keep being the good woman you are. Pray for people. But also don't be afraid to do the hard things. Nothing you face from here on in will be as painful as the pain you felt when you were poisoned and dying. It may feel strange and uncomfortable for you to sit in a church after all this time, but by doing so, you'll be sharing your story with those around you and you'll make their faith even stronger. Opening up to Vardemen and Exa and the boys, that'll be hard, too, but nothing like what you've already been through.

"And Rae. I challenge you to go seek out Rae Mobley. I made no headway with her, but maybe that's because my heart was not pure of intent when I did it. When you're feeling strong enough, pray for her. Pray for her and then see if you can find her. To see you standing before her, full of the love of the Lord…You might be able to break on through and show her the light. She's in so much pain, Connie Jo, so much pain. You might be the only person in the world who can speak to the unique pain she's feeling and let her know God's love. Maybe then she can find true happiness instead of such bitterness towards everything in this world."

Connie Jo sat in silence for a minute, letting it all wash over her. Finally, she huffed loudly, reached into her pocketbook for some Kleenex and reapplied her makeup.

"How're ya doin'?" Rusty asked.

"Gotta put on my face," she said as she continued working. "A whole new face. I got work to do. There's a wedding going on outside without me and that ain't right. I have to fix myself up so I can spread the good news."

For more information please contact:
houledavenport@aol.com